MW01492364

SPARK

Chelle
Bliss
xoxo

www.chellebliss.com
CHELLE BLISS
USA TODAY BESTSELLING AUTHOR

Publisher © Bliss Ink January 12th 2021
Edited by Lisa A. Hollett
Proofread by Read By Rose & Deaton Author Services
Cover Design © Chelle Bliss
Cover Photo © Wander Aguilar

Chelle Bliss
MENOFINKED.COM

Mallory,

You may not have come from my body,
but you'll always have a piece of my heart.

You are strong. You are brave. You are wild.
Live without apology, and love without boundaries.

I couldn't be prouder of the woman you've become.
I'll love you always and forever.

PROLOGUE

NICK

Five Years Ago

I stood behind my cousin Gigi outside Lily's house, trying to hide behind her and facing the street just as she told me to. "Bitch, open the door!" she yells into the security camera hanging above the front door. "I have a surprise for you." Gigi pushes against my back, making sure I don't turn around.

"It's late, Gigi. I'm not really in the mood for company."

"Trust me, you want to see this person." Gigi's hands are away from me again, and she moves closer to the front door, the sound of her boots on the cement unmistakable. "I can pick the lock."

"Don't you dare," Lily hisses. "I'm coming down."

"Good. She's coming down," Gigi repeats like somehow having my back to the camera makes me deaf.

A few seconds later, the front door opens, and I smile,

knowing Lily's about to shit herself. Not literally, but she's always been known for being over the top when it comes to happiness.

"Wipe that sourpuss look off your face, princess, because I'm about to blow your mind." Gigi taps my back, giving me the green light to turn around.

Lily gasps. "Nick?" She covers her mouth as her eyes widen.

"Lily," I reply back, gawking at her.

Shit is off, big-time. It's October, and Lily should be finishing her final year of school, but she is here, back in our hometown and in her own house. Lily is also the most reserved of my cousins, but the girl standing in front of me has a wilder and more carefree side than I ever knew Lily could have.

"What happened to you?" I ask, thrown the hell off because Lily isn't at school.

"What happened to me?" she repeats, pressing her hand to her chest, staring at me in disbelief. "What the hell happened to you?"

"Grew up. Filled out. Became a man," I mutter. I know she isn't talking about my size, but I also know Lily is going to be as pissed as my parents about the stupid shit I did and the fact that the school kicked me out.

Lily takes education very seriously. More seriously than most people her age. Hell, more than most people at any age.

"He's clearly still the same asshole, though," Gigi teases.

"It's part of his DNA," Lily tells her. "But what the hell are you doing here?"

I swipe my palm over my face and lift a shoulder. "School and I didn't agree anymore."

Gigi slaps me with the back of her hand, shaking her head. "He got kicked out."

Lily's eyes grow as wide as saucers. "You got kicked out?" she says softly.

I nod. "Shit happens."

"How are you still alive?" Lily asks, blinking.

After what went down, I wasn't ready to go to my parents' house. I like living, and I like breathing even more. I know if I went home, both of those could be in jeopardy.

Although my dad rarely gets pissed at me about shit, I know what went down at my swanky boarding school is going to make him blow a gasket and possibly make breathing a whole lot harder if he clocks me right in the face.

He isn't violent. Never laid a hand on me. It isn't his style. But every man has a breaking point, and I fear that getting kicked out for breaking the law isn't going to be something my father celebrates.

I follow my cousin into Lily's house, complimenting her on her place and waiting for them to lay into me.

Gigi already started on the way over here. Question after question, she hurled in my direction, grilling me like she's been trained by my father or Uncle James.

"Do your parents know you're here?" Lily asks, walking next to me toward the living room.

"Not yet, but they will tomorrow."

"Well, shit," Lily mutters, making my body jolt with her easy and carefree use of profanity.

"Sit, Nicholas." Gigi pats the spot next to her where she's collapsed onto the couch. "You have a lot of explaining to do."

As soon as I sit, Lily sits too, but on the other side of me, caging me in. "Spill the beans," she tells me, folding her leg underneath herself. "What the hell happened?"

I sit back, letting out a long, exasperated exhale. "I was running a side hustle and got caught. Simple as that."

Lily's lips flatten as she crosses her arms, tilting her head, waiting for more.

"I guess making and selling fake IDs is not only against school policy, but also against the law. I begged for mercy and leniency, but they told me to fuck off." I shrug one shoulder, my lips snarling. "Especially after Malcolm Harrison was found drunk and passed out, my well-crafted ID in his pocket. The asshole was told to either give up his supplier or get kicked out. The rat sang like a canary, I got the boot, and he's recovering in his room back in North Carolina."

Lily's mouth drops open. "You sold fake IDs?"

I grin, loving shocking my little cousin. She was always so innocent. While the rest of us were doing dumb shit all the time, she had a perfectly placed angel halo hanging above her head.

"Made them too," I tell her.

She rolls her eyes, annoyed with me as always. "Your dad is going to straight up murder you."

"He'll be pissed for a minute, but he'll get over it," I lie, waving off her comment.

"You're so dead, Nick." Gigi tips her head back and laughs. "So, so dead."

I laugh, pretending she's being dramatic but knowing she's not. I haven't seen my girls in over a year, and they haven't changed a lick physically. But in other ways, they've both gone off the deep end, and from what they're telling me about Tamara, so did she.

Lily, the little bookworm who was studying to be a doctor, dropped out of college to become a piercer at Inked, our family-run tattoo and piercing shop. Somehow, she hooked up with Jett Michaels, one of the most notorious players back in the day, and got him to settle down. I don't know how I feel about that either because I never pictured Lily with someone who's had more pussy than people have fingers and toes combined. I always pictured her losing her virginity to another virgin because she wasn't the most sexually open person I'd ever known.

Gigi, on the other hand, always had some wild in her, and she fell for a biker wannabe. They both work at Inked but met months earlier.

My other cousin, Tamara, is in her final year at college and is still on track to graduate. Over the last year, she somehow got wrapped up with more than one guy at an MC and has fallen in love with a real badass biker, shocking the shit out of everyone. Not that she found herself a hell-raising type of guy, but that she loves him and isn't already looking for an exit.

My head is spinning with the news when the front door opens and my father stands there, holding up an older Jett Michaels.

Fuck.

I crouch down, hoping to stay out of his line of sight, but only a few seconds pass before his eyes land on me.

"What. The. Fuck?" my dad hisses, finally lifting his eyes, spotting me frozen on the couch. "Am I seeing shit, or is my kid in your living room?"

I jump up from the couch, knowing shit is about to go sideways, and smash my shin into the coffee table, almost knocking it over. "I can explain."

Damn. I had hoped to get in one night's sleep before my father found out, lost his mind, I begged for mercy, and somehow, we get past this.

"Get your ass in the car," my dad bites out, low and slow.

"Catch y'all later," I say as I move toward the door, avoiding getting within arm's reach of my father.

"Bye, Nicky. Don't die!" Gigi calls out, being funny and a total asshole.

"You're going to wish for death," my father growls as my boots touch the cement outside the door.

I pick up speed, walking double time toward his car, debating on running back to my parents' instead of driving back with him.

"Don't even think about it," Dad snarls like he's reading my mind.

Busted.

I give up any thoughts of running because I'm too far from anywhere and he'll really want to beat my ass if I do.

There's no eye contact as we both open the car doors. No talking either. I slide into the seat of his car, pinning my body against the door as Dad climbs in next to me.

"Don't speak," he tells me as he fires up the engine. "Not a fucking word."

So, this is going well.

He's not yelling at me, and he hasn't grabbed me, trying to shake some sense into my thick skull either. So far, I'd call that a win.

He drives down the dark roads faster than usual, taking turns a little sharper than he normally does, too. Nothing is said the entire way home, but about a mile away from the house, he yanks the wheel to the right, pulls off to the side, and cuts the engine.

My entire body freezes, and I stop breathing, bracing myself for whatever comes next.

"What happened? And I want the truth because you know I'll be talking to the headmaster tomorrow."

I exhale, running my hands down my jeans, and lay it out without looking at him. "I was making IDs for some of the kids at school. One kid got popped. He sang. I got booted."

Even in the dark, I can feel his eyes trained on me.

"You were selling IDs?" he says, no disbelief in his voice. The words are even and low.

"Yeah."

"Fuck me," he mutters. "Your mother is going to have my balls."

I gaze across the small space, watching him shake his head in the soft glow from the dashboard.

"I should've never taught you that shit," he continues, pinching the bridge of his nose. "She's going to rip me a new asshole first, and then she's going to come after you."

I'm not sure who I'm more scared of, my mom or my dad. Dad's bigger and definitely has a hard edge to him, but Mom... Mom can turn on a dime, especially when you're acting a fool and in the wrong.

Dad has a lot of gray areas to him. His time in law enforcement taught him skills he's carried over into his work at his security and private investigation firm.

But Mom, she is all about right and wrong, and there is no in-between. Either you messed up or you were in the right, and she'd go down swinging to defend the wronged party. I know where I stand in this instance, especially in her mind.

"I'll talk to her, Dad. She won't be too upset," I lie.

"She won't be too upset?" he asks, his voice going all high-pitched with the last word. "Son, have you forgotten exactly who and how your mother is?"

I shake my head. "She's pretty hard to forget."

He closes his eyes, fingers wrapped around the

steering wheel, and inhales deeply. "We have to let the chips fall where they may. No other option."

I raise my eyebrows. Am I getting a pass? I broke the law, Dad was about to kill me, but now, he seems to think we're both going to fall on the proverbial sword to get the bad news over with.

"Don't think you're getting off scot-free with me either," he tells me, opening his eyes again and turning his body so he's facing me. "Your ass is in school by Monday, you will get straight A's this year, and you're grounded until graduation."

"But—"

"Shut it, Nick."

I clamp my mouth closed because there's no winning this argument. The only thing I can do is wait for the dust to settle, hoping they eventually take mercy on my teenage soul.

"Buckle up, kid. We're about to have a very bumpy night."

"Fuckin' great," I mumble into the darkness.

Five minutes later, I walk through the doorway of my parents' house, and Mom's standing in the foyer, arms crossed, face pinched, waiting.

Looks like Headmaster Quinlinn already called her and informed her of my permanent exit from campus.

"Couch. Now," she orders, tipping her head toward the living room with her eyes trained only on me.

I don't say a word, don't even bother pleading my

case as I toe off my boots before heading toward the couch for the ass-reaming of the century.

"Baby," Dad says, his tone very different than it was in the car. He's trying to cover his ass, buttering her up. "Maybe we should talk before—"

"No, Thomas," she cuts him off. "We're going to talk now. All three of us. Get your ass in the living room and sit next to *your* son."

I grimace, my steps slowing.

She said *your* son. That only happens when she is at maximum pissed off, and based on everything I've seen so far, she's been there for a while.

I am screwed.

Goodbye, senior year. Hello, home confinement.

1

NICK

FIVE YEARS LATER

I LOVE TACOS.

Not any kind of tacos, but the type where you sink your teeth into that crispy shell and the grease runs down your chin, puddling on the paper.

There is only one place in town where I can get my fix. It doesn't matter that it is after midnight, I am getting the damn tacos, the grease, and all the goodness.

I park my bike and stalk up to the window outside the converted ice cream joint which now serves the most slammin' Mexican within fifty miles. I'm behind a drunk guy who's ordering a shitload of food and swaying back and forth like the ground is moving underneath him.

I glance around, crossing my arms, and zero in on a pretty girl, jamming nachos into her mouth, crying in between each bite.

Not my chick. Not my problem.

Besides her, me, and the workers, the only other

person here is the drunk guy. He's leaning against the counter at the closed register window next to me, talking to himself in tongues.

"One sec." The woman on the other side of the glass and wearing a sombrero holds up a finger.

The damn hat is twice as big as her head, pink and yellow woven together, and has cotton balls hanging from the edges that shake every time she moves. When she finally glances up from the cash register and makes eye contact, she says, "Well, hey there, handsome." Her eyes move away from my face and hungrily trail down my chest and then sweep back up my arms before her face breaks out in a smile. "What can I get you tonight?"

"Five tacos with extra meat and a bottle of water." I reach into my back pocket, not looking to flirt with the sombrero girl, and grab my wallet.

I came here for tacos, not pussy.

And even if I were in the mood for pussy, she isn't my type, and it has nothing to do with the sombrero.

"A guy like you looks like he could go for something... bigger," she flirts, her voice all breathless and flirty.

"Only the five," I tell her, not wanting to be rude and definitely not wanting in her pants.

"A girl can dream," she breathes as she punches the buttons on the register. "That'll be $15.70."

I toss a twenty on the counter and hold up my hand. "Keep the change," I tell her, figuring she deserves a tip for working this shit shift, dealing with drunk idiots like the guy who ordered in front of me.

She snatches the bill off the counter, staring at my face and no longer my body. "Thanks, big guy. It's my first tip of the night, and I've been here five hours."

"People suck," I offer, rubbing the back of my neck and hoping to make an exit as quickly as possible.

"They do." She turns her back, yelling something in Spanish to the guys working in the kitchen. When she turns back, the smile is on her face again. "It'll be a minute. The dumb shits are slow tonight. Sorry."

"No worries," I tell her, stepping back. "I got nothing but time."

"You can take a seat, and I'll call you when your order is ready," she says, making change from the money I gave her and stashing it in her pocket instead of the empty tip jar.

Now I have a dilemma.

Do I sit at the table closest to the drunk guy rambling to himself or the chick who's crying in her nachos like her dog just died?

I look back and forth between the two and pick the chick because the guy isn't something I want to deal with. He is talkative, although he is only talking to himself, but I'm not about to risk that changing any time soon.

The safer option is the chick who hasn't bothered to look up from her nachos, is continuing to cry, and hasn't stopped eating. Between those tears and her chewing, the likelihood she is going to try to chat me up is slim to fuckin' none, so I pick her.

As soon as my ass hits the wood, the drunk guy, still

swaying, breaks out in song like he is performing for a crowd at a stadium.

"Christ," I mutter, shaking my head.

"Jimbo," the sombrero girl says, leaning over the counter, stretching her neck to see him. "You didn't drive here, did you?"

He shakes his head. "Walked, babe. No license, remember?"

"Only making sure." She nods, pushing his bag of food out for him to grab. "Need a ride home?"

His head shake is immediate. "It's the type of night where you need to take in the stars."

"Shitshow," I mumble, rubbing my forehead and avoiding the tragic disaster of a human being in front of me.

"Don't be watching those stars while you're walking, Jimbo. Liable to end up in a ditch or hit by a car if your head is tipped upward, drunk, and not watching where you're going."

"God will show me the way," he answers, digging into his bag with one hand and pulling out a taco.

Sombrero girl narrows her eyes and twists her thin lips. "God wants you at home so you can be at church tomorrow and not late for your daddy's sermon."

Preacher's kid. Not surprising. 'Round here, they go one of two ways. Devout or rebellious. Based on Jimbo's current situation, he is stuck somewhere in the middle. He is a believer but has different feelings on God than his father probably taught him.

"I'm never late, Tina Marie." He sways as he backs away from the building and gazes upward with his first bite. "I'm right where God meant me to be."

"Lord have mercy," the sombrero girl, Tina Marie, mutters, watching Jimbo with her eyebrows disappearing up and under the brim of the hat. She does a quick sign of the cross, mumbling under her breath until something behind her takes her attention away from the taco-eating, stargazing guy who's wandering down the side of the highway.

The crying chick is still crying, or at least, she is until her phone rings.

"What?" she snaps, sounding more vicious than sad.

"Where the hell are you?" the guy asks through the speaker.

"Go fuck yourself."

"Bitch, I want an answer," he roars.

I wince, not liking the name nor the tone in which he's speaking to her, but I remain forward-facing.

Not my chick. Not my business.

"Get. Your. Fucking. Ass. Back. To. The. Hotel," he says slowly, pausing between each word.

"Let me lay this out for you," she snaps, the wood creaking on her picnic bench as she shifts her weight.

I want to turn around. I want to watch her because, based on her tone, she is not going to get her fucking ass back to anywhere the asshole is at, and I think she's about to clue him the fuck in.

"I'm. Not. Coming. Back. You. Fucking. Cheating.

Bastard," she replies exactly the same way he spoke to her, emphasizing every single word.

He grunts. "Jo, I'm done playing. Your skinny little ass better be back in my hotel room in the next thirty minutes, or there's going to be hell to pay."

She chuckles, but not because the shit is funny, but because the cheating bastard is delusional.

I've heard that tone more times than I care to remember coming from my cousins—Gigi, Tamara, and Lily—and it is never followed by anything good.

"Maybe you should find that blond bimbo you had spread out on my bed with your face buried between her legs. Call her and boss her skinny ass around, because this bitch... She isn't coming back."

"When I find you," he warns, his voice low and growly, "I'm going to make..."

Then his voice stops, and there's silence.

"Fuck him."

I brace, waiting for the crying to start again, and right on cue, it does.

"He ain't worth it," I tell her, keeping my back to her, giving her privacy even though she laid out her business in front of me, the sombrero girl, and whatever creatures are moving around at this hour.

"Excuse me?" she asks, and it's not in that sweet way that makes my balls tight.

I turn, figuring she at least deserves my eyes when I reply. "He ain't worth it."

Her eyes narrow as she wipes away the stray tears

running down her face. "I don't know who the fuck you think—"

I lift my hand, stopping her from laying into me like she did the guy on the phone. "Babe. It's none of my business. Or at least it wasn't until you put that shit on speakerphone and decided to share with the world."

She peers around, probably noticing it's only us and the chick with the hat, but she remains silent as I keep talking.

In the dim lighting, I can clearly see she's pretty, even with the puffy eyes and slick cheeks. She has long blond hair, piled high on her head in a messy bun with a few pieces falling free like they need to breathe. Her nose is slender and straight, clearly never having been broken before. Her cheeks are high, almost touching her light blue eyes, which are staring right at me.

"But I've been sitting here for five minutes, listening to you cry. Figured something bad happened. Had your heart broken or some shit. But there's no man in the world who talks to you like that and does shit like he did who's worth those tears."

Her back straightens as she licks the cheese sauce off her fingers, drawing my attention away from her swollen eyes to her plump lips. "You don't know me."

I nod, tapping my fingers against the worn wood of the table. "You're right, I don't know you. But I know women. Have a whole family filled with them. Someone talks to them the way that asshole talked to you, he doesn't talk again for a few months."

She blinks, gawking at me. "He doesn't talk for a few months?" she questions, blinking quicker.

I hold up my fist. "This is my asshole muter."

She tilts her head, staring at my closed fist, still blinking. "You have an asshole muter?"

I smile, pointing at my hand. "Been muting assholes since Tony Mandello called my cousin a slut after getting in her pants. He was almost twice my size and a handful of years older, but he was eating through a straw for months, regretting those words."

"You broke his jaw?" she gasps, eyebrows up.

"He was a dick and deserved sucking down a cheeseburger like a milk shake for what he said and how he treated her. These douchebags aren't worth the tears."

She smacks her hands together, righting herself. "I'm not crying because of Jamison."

I scrunch my nose.

"What?" she asks, immediately crossing her arms.

"Jamison." I snort, rolling my eyes. "Total pussy name."

"It's the perfect name for a cheating bastard."

"It's the perfect name for a man who barely has a dick, doesn't know how to use it, and doesn't care to satisfy anyone other than himself."

She blinks again, staring at me in shock, and my gaze dips down to that perfect pouty mouth of hers again. "Four inches."

"Four inches what?" I ask, moving my eyes back to hers.

"His dick is four inches."

I rock backward, figuring he had SDS, Small Dick Syndrome, but not realizing he was that fucking small. I snort again, but this time louder.

"And thin." She holds up her pinkie finger and waves it. "Like super thin."

"Tragic," I mutter, shaking my head. "And you dealt with that shit?"

"Obviously, I was the one lacking since he needed to plant his face between the maid's legs," she says sarcastically. "Between his small dick, temper, and cheating, I'd say I got the better end of this breakup."

"You sure as fuck did. So, stop the tears, yeah?"

She stares at me for a minute, blinking a few times, no doubt making judgments about me. Every single one of them is probably wrong too. "What's your name?"

"Nick."

"You live around here?"

"Nope," I lie because Jo seems like trouble and tragedy, two things I didn't come here for.

"Damn," she whispers.

I hold up my hand, knowing I'll regret this moment for the rest of my life. "You need a man, baby?" I ask her, my gaze dropping to the rise of her tits, glistening in the dim moonlight, covered in her tears.

"I think I've had enough men for a while, but I need a place to crash, and you seem like a really nice guy."

I bark out a laugh. "One. I'm not nice. I'm not Jamison, but sweet is not me. Two. I have one bed, and no one sleeps in it except me. Three. I don't fuck random chicks who've been crying over the loss of four-inch dick within the last five minutes."

Her head jerks back like I slapped her with my honesty. She recovers quickly and leans forward, placing her palms flat on the table. "Well, aren't you a wordy prick. Now, let me explain a few things to you, because we don't know each other, but you've clearly already formed an opinion. One. I don't need a bed. The couch will be fine."

I laugh and her eyes narrow. "Babe, you're too classy for a couch. I'm sure you lie on seven-hundred-thread-count sheets, pillows of real feathers, and that high-tech body-sculpting mattress bullshit too."

She wrinkles her nose. "Asshole," she mumbles.

"Not making me want to change my mind."

She steals my move and holds up her hand, wanting me to shut the fuck up, so I do. "Two. You don't look sweet, nor do you talk sweet. I may seem like whatever, but I can assure you, your opinion of me is wrong too."

"Nor," I tease, still laughing. "Who the fuck says nor?"

She gives me the middle finger. "Three. I don't fuck guys who use their fists as a mute button. I also don't fuck random dudes I meet at taco stands after midnight in the middle of bumfucking nowhere. I'm not thirsty for cock—'specially not starving for your dick, baby," she says that last word so sweetly that if I weren't listening to the entire lecture, I'd think she liked me.

"Then there's nothing more to say," I tell her. "We're both agreed."

She throws up her hands and stands. "You know what?"

"What, babe?" I ask, genuinely curious where this crazy-ass chick is going to take the conversation next.

"Never mind, jagoff." She waves her hand at me and storms off, leaving her half-eaten nachos on the table. "You can go fuck yourself too!" she yells across the parking lot without looking back.

"After the tacos," I reply to no one as she stalks toward a car parked in the shadows where the lights don't hit.

"Order's ready," Tina Marie calls out, craning her neck toward the parking lot as the engine to the crazy chick's sweet ride roars to life.

I stand and move toward the counter, grabbing my tacos.

Jo backs out, almost nailing my bike with her overpriced black luxury car and fishtails out of the parking lot before I make it back to the table.

"Tacos are so much easier than pussy," I mutter to myself, unwrapping the first taco.

For ten minutes, I sit in pure silence, relishing the crispy goodness without listening to a crying chick or a dumb-ass drunk. Not giving two fucks about the grease running down my chin because no one's watching or bothering me anymore.

As soon as I'm done, I throw my trash and Jo's in the

nearby can, leaving the place how I found it, minus the crying girl with tons of attitude and a mouth that could suck a man dry in minutes.

Back on my bike, heading toward home, I don't make it five miles when I hit the first traffic light.

Fuck.

If you hit one, you hit them all unless you haul ass, breaking the cycle. I turn my head to the right, continuing to curse under my breath when I see it.

The sleek black car Jo sped off in is under a light in a virtually empty superstore parking lot.

Not my chick. Not my business.

The light turns green, and I'm off before I let that voice in the back of my skull tell me to get my head out of my ass and make sure she's okay.

I already know she has no hotel room to go back to. And based on where she is, which is my hometown, there isn't a decent hotel for at least fifty miles. Add in the fact that it is after midnight in the middle of nowhere, and I know she is stuck.

Fuck me.

"Always look out for a woman, Nicky." My father's words echo in my head. "It's our job to protect them."

"Goddamn it," I grumble as I make a U-turn, heading back to do what's right, even if it kills me.

2

NICK

I PULL INTO THE DARKNESS, A COUPLE DOZEN FEET away, and watch her as she reclines the seat, curls onto her side, and closes her eyes.

I glance up, cursing. I can't leave her out here to sleep, but I'm also tired, and I know with her around, I'm not getting a wink of sleep.

I exhale, climbing off my bike and stalking toward her car, hoping I won't regret my next move for the rest of my life.

I knock lightly against the driver's side window with my knuckles. "Jo," I call.

Her eyes snap open, but she doesn't move. She stares at me, wide-eyed. "What in the fuck," she gasps, or at least I think she does since I can't hear her but am reading her lips instead.

"Babe." I motion toward the glass. "Roll it down."

She blinks, her hand still tucked under her cheek,

lying on her side. "Go away!" she yells loud enough for me to make out those words clear as day.

"Come on," I plead, stepping back and running my hand through my hair, trying to play it cool. "We gotta talk."

A second later, she sits up and grabs the steering wheel with one hand and gives me the middle finger with the other.

This bitch is dripping with attitude.

"You can't stay here."

Her eyes narrow as she finally cracks the window, but only enough so she can tell me, "You don't own this place. Get the fuck out of here."

I stifle my laughter. Her attitude doesn't scare me. Growing up Gallo, I don't have a woman in my family who isn't filled with piss and vinegar and wouldn't make Jo seem like a kitten compared to her. "I know I don't fucking own the place, but you still can't stay here."

"Fuck off," she replies, saying those words calmly, evenly, and softly. "Like, all the way off."

"All the way off?" I ask, making sure I heard her right. "How far do the fucks go?"

She stares at me, her lips flat, blinking. "Are you for real?"

"Real as they come, babe." I smile. "But listen to me, you really can't stay here. I'm not giving you shit, but it's not safe. And if the homeless don't bother you, the cops sure as fuck will."

"I'm too tired to drive back to Clearwater. It's over an

hour away. I checked my phone, and there's one motel—they rent by the hour, by the way—and right now, they're booked. So, since I have nowhere to go, I'm exhausted, and my eyes are so damn puffy, I'll take my chances with the cops and the homeless."

I brush my fingers back and forth through my hair. "You don't know me, and I don't know you, but other than being an emotional wreck with a mouth like a truck driver, I'm pretty sure you're not going to whack me in the middle of the night."

She raises an eyebrow. "Only pretty sure?"

I nod. "If you tried, I know I can take you, but that's beside the point. My place is a few miles down the road, and you can crash there tonight and head back to Jamison tomorrow."

"I'm not going back to Jamison."

"Well then, you can go wherever the hell you want tomorrow."

She eyes me, studying my face, passing judgment on me. "How do I know you're not a murderer?"

I point to the camera on the light post next to her car. "Cameras everywhere, babe. If I were going to do you harm, I sure as hell wouldn't leave any evidence."

"How is that even your answer?"

"Babe."

She shakes her head. "I didn't notice the cameras, but somehow you've already seen them, knew you were spotted, and decided to share that information with me."

"My dad's ex-law enforcement. He's taught me how

to survey a situation and always be aware of my surroundings. But besides that, doesn't everyone know there're cameras always watching, especially in parking lots and high-crime areas?"

She looks around. "This is a high-crime area?"

My hometown isn't much. One busy street packed with retail chains and restaurants. Every other inch consists of housing developments or acreage with "No Trespassing" signs posted on the gate at the end of their driveway. I may have exaggerated about the high-crime area. We've never had much action when it comes to shit like that. The town is too small, and everyone knows everyone's face and, therefore, their business.

"My place is a hell of a lot safer than here," I tell her, wondering why the hell I'm working so hard with someone who's clearly in need but doesn't want my help. "But if you'd rather—"

"No." The window moves a few inches lower. "I wouldn't rather stay here."

"Then fire her up, and let's get a move on," I tell her, ticking my chin toward the car.

"I need to tell someone where I am. Just to be safe."

I reach into my pocket, fishing out my wallet, and I slide out my driver's license and hold it out for her. "Send my info to someone and tell them to check on you tomorrow."

She plucks the plastic card from my fingers, her eyes running over the information. "Nicholas Gallo," she reads.

"Babe, snap the picture, send the message, and let's go. I want to get home and get some shut-eye before I have to be at work tomorrow."

She raises her hand and turns on the overhead light. "Fine," she mutters. "But I'm not having sex with you. I want that to be clear."

"Clear as fucking day. I thought we agreed on that fact back at the taco joint. I know you think you're all that, but you're not my type."

Her brows furrow. "I'm not your type?"

"Jesus fuckin' Christ. Take the damn photo and follow me," I tell her, stalking away, heading back to my bike.

Tomorrow, I'm going to tell my dad he's a damn fool. Not every woman in the world needs to be protected, especially not difficult ones who clearly do not want help.

By the time my ass is on my bike, her engine roars to life and her headlights turn on.

Thank fuck.

She follows me out of the parking lot, keeping her distance as we drive down the main road, turning onto my street. Her car slows, the space between my bike and her car growing wider.

I cut the engine, rolling my bike into my driveway and walking it up to the garage door. My neighbor, Mrs. Marcum, is a light sleeper, and her baby an even lighter one. The last thing I need is her banging on my door in the morning, telling me what a shit human I am for waking up her baby in the middle of the night.

Jo pulls behind my bike, staring up at my house through the windshield, craning her neck. I put the kickstand down, climb off, and motion for her to move her ass too.

She climbs out slowly, her eyes sweeping across the exterior of my house. "This is where you live?" she asks without looking at me.

"Uh, yeah. Not what you expected?"

She lifts her purse higher on her shoulder. "I figured you'd live in a..."

"Shithole?" I finish her thought for her.

She winces. "Well, no. But not something so...normal."

"I may not need seven-hundred-thread-count sheets, but I like my space, and that includes a nice house."

She twists, looking around the neighborhood. "I figured you more for an apartment or downtown loft type of guy."

I laugh. "Sweetheart, did you see a downtown loft anywhere for me to even live in if I were that type of guy, which I'm not?"

She shakes her head.

"Can we go in now?" I ask her, seeing as she hasn't moved an inch away from her car door. "I'm tired, and standing out here having a conversation for the entire neighborhood to hear really isn't my thing."

"They can hear us?"

"I installed security cams, which include speakers, on every house on this block. They see and hear everything."

She wrinkles her nose. "You did that?"

"Yep."

"Why?"

"Security."

"From all the criminals?" she stammers, clutching her purse to her side.

"From whatever. Ain't any bad shit in this neighborhood because we make sure there's no bad shit. It's the modern-day version of community watch. Eyes and ears everywhere."

"Figured out here everyone sat in their windows with their shotguns, waiting for the bad to come to them."

I laugh. "Total city girl."

"You say that like it's a bad thing."

"It ain't. Now, let's go. Cameras, remember?" I remind her, and that gets her ass moving, slamming her door and heading toward me.

"Well, come on." She shoos me toward the door. "Wouldn't want all the prying eyes to have something to gossip about tomorrow."

I shake my head, walking in front of her. "You will not be gossip."

"I'm sure I'm not the first woman you've brought home."

"Won't be the last either," I mumble into the door as the lock disengages.

She stays five feet away from my back but follows me inside. "Here," she says.

I turn, spotting my license in her hand, and take it

back. "I'll grab you some blankets and pillows. No feathers, though," I tease, turning on the lights as I move down the hallway. "You should be comfortable enough to get a few hours of sleep."

She stands in the entry, not having moved more than a few feet inside the house. "Why are you helping me?"

"My dad always taught me to help others, especially women, when they're in need. And if I've ever met anyone in need, it's you, babe."

"I hate that." She scrunches up her nose again.

"Hate what?" I pull down a pile of blankets and pillows, carrying as many as I possibly can, hoping something will satisfy the city girl.

"Babe."

"Well, it's a good thing you won't be here long enough to have to hate it much longer. Mean no disrespect with the word."

"I mean, I've been called worse, but it's just so...archaic."

"I'm a man. I make no apologies for that."

She sighs, following me into the living room when her feet finally come unstuck from the tile. "The inside is prettier than the outside," she says, her eyes moving around the room, soaking in my space.

I drop the pile of pillows and blankets on the love seat before starting to prep the couch for her. I have two spare bedrooms, neither of which are set up for company, and that's done on purpose. "I don't know what kind of men you've been with. Don't know where you come from.

Don't care either. But babe shouldn't make your face twist up like it does. Especially not when you have a douchebag like Janison."

"Jamison," she corrects me. "Like the whiskey but spelled differently."

"Whatever," I mutter, tossing the pillows on one end and covering the couch with another blanket. "Bathroom's down the hall. You need anything, don't wake me up. I got nothing to hide. You need water, get it. You need to piss, go. You're hungry, good luck because all I have is frozen shit, chips, and some granola bars."

"I'll be fine," she insists, standing stock-still, staring at me. "Thank you."

"Pains you to say that, doesn't it?" I tease, giving her a smile.

"No," she lies.

"You wanna get out of that?" I ask as my gaze dips to her shorts and lacy tank top.

"I can sleep in this."

"I have an old T-shirt and shorts that might fit you."

"I'm fine," she tells me again, setting her purse down on the coffee table right in front of the pillows. "If I could sleep in my car, I'm pretty damn sure I can handle a couch in my shorts."

"Suit yourself," I mutter, walking away. "Night."

"That's it?" she asks.

I turn my head, glancing over my shoulder, and raise an eyebrow. "You want something else?"

"Well. I...no."

"Good."

"I only figured..."

"Babe, I'm tired. Can we save the chitchat for a time when I'm not seeing double, dead on my feet, with five tacos in my belly weighing me down?"

She nods. "Night."

"Night, babe," I say, throwing in another babe because she hates it.

She mutters something to herself, no doubt calling me an asshole along with an entire slew of curse words.

I kick off my boots, strip out of my shirt and pants as soon as I'm inside my room, and climb into bed. I give no shits there's a chick down the hall. Hot or not, I don't want a piece of her and whiskey's trouble.

My eyes are barely closed when her cell phone goes off, the ringer set so loud it could wake the dead.

"I don't know where I am," she tells the person on the phone. "I mean, I know the address, but I don't know where in the hell in Florida I am." There's a long pause. "I started driving, headed north until the city lights fell away." Another long pause. "I don't know what I was thinking. Clearly, I wasn't, but he offered me a place to stay, and it was either this or a parking lot."

The hardwood floor creaks, and I know she's on the move, pacing back and forth in the living room.

"He seems really nice, though." A few seconds go by before she starts talking again, and I lie in the darkness, waiting for her next words. "He told me to send you his information in case. I don't think a criminal would do that, Kimberly."

Jo laughs, the sweet sound echoing down the hallway. "I highly doubt he's a sex trafficker. Stop with your nonsense. I'm too tired to get into it with you. Let me call you in the morning, and we'll talk about what to do with Jamison."

What to do with Jamison? I'm not sure what that means, but he deserves to be dropped on his ass for the way he talks to her, along with what he did to her. I've known so many chicks like her, and she'll probably be back in his arms tomorrow night, willing to forgive him for anything.

"Kimberly, I got this." There's a short pause, and the floor quiets along with her mouth. "I have my Mace, and if he tries anything, I won't hesitate to use it."

3

JO

Bacon. The smell is unmistakable. For a moment, I lie there dazed and confused.

Shit.

I'm not at home. I'm not even at the hotel room Jamison booked for us on the beach.

I glance around as last night comes slamming back into me.

Jamison and the maid.

Me storming out.

My drive to the middle of nowhere.

The taco stand.

Nachos.

Tears.

Jamison's phone call.

A hot but nosy guy.

The same hot guy who was also a macho asshole, but also kind of sweet.

Trying to catch some sleep in my car because my stupid ass drove to who-the-fuck-knows-where Florida.

The same kind of sweet asshole finding me in the parking lot of some random store and offering me a place to sleep.

And somehow, God only knows why, I agreed to go to his house.

I mean, I know why. My rental car is expensive and foreign, but in no way is it comfortable. Also, I didn't exactly feel safe from prying eyes and passersby as I lay in the parking lot, try to sleep and failing.

That all led me to here.

Sleeping on the couch of the hot, sweet jerk, still in the middle of nowhere, but alive and almost rested.

I peer down, lifting the blanket, making sure I still have on my clothes.

Anything could've happened while I was sleeping. I took a sleeping pill last night. Probably not the smartest thing to do, but I couldn't get settled.

I take a minute to look around the room I barely had time to take in last night before he threw some blankets down and left me alone, not giving two shits if I was a murderer or a thief.

I'm not either, but I could've been, and he didn't seem to care one way or the other. That's the luxury of having a penis and not being in the public eye.

The living room is nicely decorated. Nothing feminine, but clean lines without an ounce of color except black and white.

A well-worn black leather chair is next to the couch, with a chrome-and-glass coffee in front of the two, rounding out the ensemble. Everything is neat and organized, which is more than I can say about my place in LA or Jamison's, for that matter.

"You eat eggs?"

I bite my lip, lying perfectly still, hoping he'll carry on without me.

Play dead. I could do that. I've done it before, and it's always worked. I have the ability to hold my breath longer than most Olympic swimmers. I could fool him, right?

Duh, Jo.

Play dead too well and he may call the police, which would then lead to an ambulance, which would then lead to too many people asking too many questions.

The last thing I want to do is make small talk with a stranger over breakfast in day-old clothes with makeup that no doubt has smeared down my face, making me look like something out of a horror movie.

"Babe, heard you move. I know you're awake. Stop fuckin' around. You want eggs or something else?" he asks again, this time standing over me, eyes studying me as I lie as still as a statue, but my eyes are wide open.

I lift my gaze to him and narrow my eyes. "Scrambled with cheese and ketchup."

Holy mother of God.

In the darkness last night, I could tell he was cute, even if I did have blurry vision from the stupid tears filling my eyes. But in the daylight...in the daylight, he is...

He winces, holding a spatula in one hand and a pan in the other, giving me a super-judgy look. "That's criminal."

I roll my eyes as I sit up, avoiding his stare and needing to look away instead of gawking at the insanely hot and shirtless man standing over me. "You asked. I answered," I throw back, sounding snotty as hell.

"Suit yourself," he grunts before the sound of his boots against the hardwood grows softer, and I finally allow myself to breathe.

He didn't ask me a million questions, never even tried anything remotely indecent, and he is making me breakfast. Eggs, to be exact. Something no man I've ever dated has done for me before. I need to put my attitude aside, saving it for the real person I am pissed at—and that man is Jamison.

I stand up and turn to face where the sound of his footsteps went. For a moment, I'm stunned and motionless. The kitchen is more beautiful and immaculate than the living room. Shiny black cabinets with white stone countertops. Totally manly.

He peers in my direction as he stands in front of the stove, looking like he does this every day. My mouth is suddenly dry as I soak him in, shirtless and covered in muscles and sporting a massive back tattoo, with his pants slung low on his hips.

"Toast?" he asks, giving his attention back to the pan and taking it away from me.

Fucking hell.

The man may not talk in complete sentences, but his body is smokin' hot. Jamison, on the other hand, is tall, thin, and not a single piece of ink. He is willowy and athletic, but in no way would I describe him as ripped. This guy, though... has the entire package.

When I don't answer, he turns his deep blue eyes back to me.

I swallow, suddenly dumb struck and mute.

"Toast," he repeats, smirking. "Bread. Do you eat it?"

I nod, not speaking.

"Wheat?"

I nod again because I'm a freaking moron.

Beautiful men with hot bodies aren't new to me. But based on the way I'm acting, it's as if I've never seen anything like him before.

"Bathroom?" I squeak out, somehow finding my voice lodged somewhere in my vagina.

He ticks his head to the right. "Down the hall. Second door on the right."

I grab my phone off the coffee table and make a beeline for the bathroom, needing to check in with Kimberly. When I turn on my screen, I have five missed text messages, all from her and none from Jamison.

Thank God.

Kimberly (7:08 a.m.): Are you okay?

Kimberly (7:15 a.m.): I'm worried.

Kimberly (7:21 a.m.): Bitch, I'm texting you.

Kimberly (7:31 a.m.): Maybe I should call the police and send them to Nick's.

Ahh. That's right. I'd forgotten his name in the haze of last night. Thank God for her.

Kimberly (7:33 a.m.): I'm getting ready to call the cops. Last chance.

My eyes widen.

If the cops are about to beat on his door, it's because my publicist is completely insane.

I dial her immediately, and on the very first ring, she answers. "What in the fuck is wrong with you?" she yells into the phone, almost blowing out my eardrum. "I've been up all night worrying about you."

"I'm fine. Thanks," I say sarcastically.

"Jo, I've been texting you for over a half hour. What in the fuck have you been doing? I thought he killed you and I was too late to save your life."

"You seriously need to stop watching so many crime shows. Not everyone is a murderer."

She makes a *pfft* sound. "You clearly need to get your head out of your Hollywood ass and realize there's real life and fiction. You're not living in a fairy tale or some sappy television sitcom. Bad shit happens to good people. And bad shit happens even more to rich people who live in the public eye. That bad shit also seems to happen a lot in small towns no one has ever heard of."

"It's not that bad in this area," I lie, turning around and finding the bathroom is as lovely as the rest of the house. And like the other rooms, everything is black and white.

There's definitely a pattern. The guy is clearly afraid of color, or maybe he thinks real men only have two shades.

"His house is nice."

"Nice as in the double-wide that isn't too old, or nice as in it's not a complete shithole but made out of bricks?"

I wrinkle my nose. "What in the hell are you talking about?"

"I did an internet search of the town you're in. You know what I found?"

I lean over the counter, staring at myself in the mirror, blinking at the horrific reflection staring back at me. My mascara had streaked down my cheeks from the crying, and whatever was left on my lashes found a home under my eyes too. "What?"

"Not a goddamn fucking thing."

"What?" I repeat, confused.

"It's so ridiculous and small, there's barely anything about the place online. It's as if it doesn't even exist, and if it does, there's nothing notable there to even mention."

"They have a killer taco stand," I tell her, moving my face closer to the mirror and wiping at my eyes.

"A restaurant?"

"No. It was an old gas station or ice cream place with some wooden picnic tables, but they had really great nachos."

"Did Jamison fuck with your head that bad? Do you even hear yourself?"

I bend down, opening the cabinet under the sink, looking for a washcloth or something to wash my face. "What are you talking about? The place I ate last night that's just down the road a bit should have its own website."

"Oh God. She even talks like *them* now."

"Who's *them*?" I snap as I stand, washcloth in hand.

Jesus. I am a mess. Crying always does weird shit to my face, and it will be a few more hours before I look like myself again. I need a shower, makeup, and a change of clothes, but all of that requires heading back to the hotel and confronting Jamison.

Not happening.

"Down the road a bit? Who says that?"

"I don't know. I'd give you the exact GPS coordinates if I knew them, but I'm not awake. And you're too busy giving me a hard time instead of being happy that I'm alive and well."

Kimberly coughs. "I am happy you're alive. I was worried, especially when you didn't reply."

"I took a pill and passed out. Plus, I'm still on LA time, and the jet lag is killing me."

"How can I help?" she asks, finally doing the job I pay her for instead of mothering and chastising me.

"Nothing." I turn my face to the right, staring at my profile, waiting for the water to warm. "I'll head back to the hotel after I have breakfast."

"Breakfast?"

"He's making me eggs and toast."

"Men do not cook for strangers without a reason."

"Seriously, Kimberly, stop being a total weirdo. He was making himself something to eat and is being nice to me. He's taking pity on me and nothing else."

"Mm-hm. Trust me. He wants something. All men do."

"Wow, girl. Who did you so wrong? I'm the one who should be hating men right now, not you." I place my phone on the counter, putting her on speakerphone with the volume as low as possible so I can only barely hear her above the sound of the running water.

"No one. Someone in your position can never be too careful. He clearly knows who you are. Everyone in the country knows who you are unless they're living under a rock. Don't be stupid and fall for his bullshit." She pauses for a second as I rub some soap between my palms. "And there's no one who does anything for you without wanting something in return. And just so you know..."

I stop moving because nothing good ever follows that statement. Not when it comes to Kimberly. It's her way of letting me know there's something I need to know that I won't like.

"Yeah?" I ask, lifting my hands to my face, ready to scrub away the remnants of last night.

"The news already broke about Jamison cheating. Somehow, probably the bitch-ass maid opened her fat yap and got paid doing it, the press got ahold of the story and has been running it on television all morning."

"Fucking great," I mutter with my hands covered in soap and pressed against my cheeks. "I'm sure they're loving every juicy detail."

"Don't worry," she says, drawing the second word out for more than a few seconds. "He's the one coming off badly. He did you wrong, and all of America knows it."

I scrub the soap into my cheeks, trying not to get too close to my mouth. "You know how much I hate tabloid news, no matter how it makes me look. It's always wrong. Always blown way out of proportion."

"They said you caught him with his face buried between another woman's legs."

I don't even flinch at her words. "Sounds about right," I clip, splashing water on my face.

"Babe, eggs are done, and toast is about to pop," Nick says at the door, not knocking or caring about my privacy.

"I'll be right there," I call out, my face dripping with water as I reach for the washcloth I'd set down next to me.

"Babe?" Kimberly asks, sounding more than shocked. "What the fuck aren't you telling me?"

"Nothing." I dry my face, looking no better than I did a minute ago.

"He called you babe. No man calls a stranger babe. No one."

"He knows I hate it. So, he keeps calling me babe to piss me off."

"You watch that one. No doubt he knows who you are and would probably be more than happy to sell a story about you to the tabloids too. Watch yourself. Get out of there as soon as possible, and call me later so I don't worry all day."

"I will."

"Bye, babe," Kimberly snickers.

"Fuck off," I tell her, ending the phone call.

All of America knows Jamison cheated. I don't know what's worse. Him doing it, or everyone knowing I wasn't good enough for him and he went elsewhere—to our hotel maid—to satisfy himself.

A glutton for punishment, I open my web browser, heading to the most popular Hollywood gossip website.

Josephine Done Dirty by Her Man.

Shit.

The headline sounds so much more salacious than it really is. Done dirty could be anything. I hate tabloids and their ability to make even the victim look horrible in any situation. Kimberly told me I looked good in this one, but based on the headline alone and the general public's inability to read beyond the first six words, I do not, in fact, look good at all.

Before leaving the bathroom, I take a deep breath, hold it inside, and find my center.

I'm not going to let anyone see me crack, not even a complete stranger.

I can do this.

I did nothing wrong.

I hold my head high as I walk out of the bathroom in my day-old clothes, no makeup, hair not even remotely tame, and head toward the kitchen.

Nick has two plates on the island, side by side, with only a few inches separating us. My eggs are exactly as I'd asked, while his are all egg whites, along with wheat toast and enough bacon to feed an entire family.

He is sitting on the stool next to what is supposed to be mine. "I put the ketchup on the side because there was no way I was going to cover the protein with that shit," he says, not looking up or turning around to face me.

I slide into the seat next to him, not looking his direction as I pick up the fork, digging into the cheesy scrambled eggs and dipping them in the ketchup.

He grunts, making a sound like I've physically wounded him.

I ignore him, adding more ketchup to my first bite to piss him off. "These look great," I marvel, trying to sound grateful because I am, even if he thinks my food choices are subpar.

His gaze moves from my fork, which is covered mostly in ketchup compared to eggs, back to my eyes. "You cannot eat that shit and like it."

"I can." I smile, lifting the fork to my lips. "And I love it," I tell him.

He stares at me, not blinking, face tight as I place the fork in my mouth.

I close my lips around the tines, wishing I hadn't gone so overboard with the damn ketchup. But I couldn't help myself since he was being so damn judgy. "Mmm," I moan, closing my eyes and pretending they are the best thing I've ever eaten.

"Fuckin' unbelievable," he mutters softly. "Beautiful chick. Grossest taste."

My eyes fly open. "My taste isn't gross," I snap after I swallow down the ketchup with a dash of eggs.

"Wouldn't know good food if it hit you in that ass, babe."

"I have exquisite taste," I argue, turning up my nose and going back to stabbing at my eggs and slathering them in more ketchup.

"Not in food, and based on what I heard, not in men either."

My fork is almost to my lips when he delivers that last punch. My stomach gurgles, but not from hunger. "What did you hear?"

His blue eyes are back on me again, studying my face, forehead furrowed. "What do you mean?"

"What did you *hear*?" I repeat, not even blinking and barely breathing. "Who did you hear it from?"

He drops his fork on his plate and turns his body sideways, his knees touching my thigh. "I don't know what in the hell you're so nutty about, babe, but I was there last night when that piece of trash you call a boyfriend had words for you. I heard all the shitty things he said to you and the way he talked to you like you were nothing." He pauses, tilts his head, and stares me straight in the eyes with no expression. "Shitty taste."

"Oh." I'm a little relieved and also totally embarrassed. "I thought you heard from somewhere else."

He looks at me funny, like I have two heads. "Where would I hear? I'm pretty damn sure we have no one in common."

This tells me two important things. He has no idea who I am, and he doesn't watch television or care about celebrities. Maybe he's lying, but he seems like a pretty straight shooter.

I shrug. "I don't know. I was only asking."

My phone vibrates between our plates, Jamison's name flashing across the screen. I stare at it, my stomach turning like the eggs and ketchup are doing the hula dance inside.

"You gonna answer that?" he asks when I sit there too long, letting it ring three times.

"I don't want to," I mumble, going back to my breakfast.

"Your life," he quips as the phone continues to move across the stone countertop.

We sit in silence, eating, him grunting almost every time I lift the ketchup-covered eggs to my mouth, until my phone starts ringing again.

"You should answer," he says to me. "Tell him to fuck off."

"I can't. He's just sooo..."

"You love him?"

I scrunch my face. "No."

"You want him back?"

I shake my head. "He's a dick."

Nick nods, reaches for my phone, and taps the screen.

My eyes widen and I reach for the phone, but Nick pushes my hand away with his elbow.

"She's busy," Nick rumbles in that sexy deep voice of his before he pauses, his eyes moving to me. "Don't fuckin' worry about who I am. I know who you are, and she's done with your sorry ass. She's over you. Finished. You fucked up, and there's no going back."

I smile, watching him make faces as Jamison screams on the other end.

"Again, buddy, I don't give a fuck. And I'm pretty sure Jo doesn't give a fuck either."

I giggle and immediately cover my mouth to hide the sound. I seriously don't give a fuck about Jamison. Not after what he did.

"We'll be there in an hour, and you can say this shit to my face."

My laughter dies and my breathing stops. *We?*

"Best if you're not there when we come for her stuff," Nick warns, but he's smiling, enjoying himself.

Nick looks so much more handsome with a smile. His teeth are white and straight. He's dreamy in a rustic, blue-collar kind of way.

"If you're there, you won't talk to her, won't look at her, won't even breathe in her direction, or you're going to deal with me. Clear out, man. Admit you fucked up. Accept defeat. We're coming for her shit, and she's gone."

Nick taps the screen, drops the phone, and goes back to his breakfast like none of that happened.

"Um," I mumble, my eyes moving from him to my phone. "*We're* going to the hotel?"

"Yeah, babe. Eat those shitty ketchup eggs, and I'll help you get your things."

"Why?" I ask, my mouth hanging open.

He runs his hand across his mouth, studying me for a second. "Why not?"

"You don't know me."

"I may not know you, but I'm not letting you go back there to get your shit alone. The man is a raving lunatic. If I'm there, he won't fuck with you. You get your shit, and you're done with him. We leave, and you live your life."

"I live my life?"

He nods. "I'd hope so. Eat," he commands, nudging my arm. "We leave in ten."

"Nick." I stare at him. "Do you know who I am?"

"Don't care, babe."

"I can't go there. I can't. People will be watching."

He doesn't even blink. "Want me to handle it?"

"I don't know."

"Eat, and we'll talk on the way. You can explain whatever this code you're talking in is all about."

"Okay," I murmur and go back to my eggs, praying this all doesn't blow up in my face.

4

NICK

Jo has her feet up on the dashboard of the old pickup truck I spent three months restoring. Her head's bobbing with the music, and she's dancing in the seat, looking chill as fuck for the first time since I met her.

"You going to tell me the big secret?" I ask when we get close enough to the fancy-ass hotel she and Jamison were staying at.

"I don't really want to kill my vibe," she mutters. "And the information will most certainly do that."

"Are you going in with me, then?"

She stops moving, curling forward and flattening her body against her legs in some wicked-ass yoga move. "I can't."

"Fine, but I need only the basics, babe. Don't need your entire life story like I'm watching some afterschool special."

She turns her face toward me, her body still folded like a pretzel. "Only the basics?" she repeats.

I nod. "I need to know what I'm walking into before I walk into it."

She sighs, straightening her body again and slinking down into the passenger seat. "People are always watching me. My family is kind of well-known. There will probably be ten photographers camped somewhere outside the hotel lobby, waiting for me to show up to snap my picture to make money."

I rub the back of my neck with one hand, the fingers of my other gripping the steering wheel. "I attract all the crazies," I mutter into the windshield.

"I'm not crazy, Nick. You'll see."

I move my gaze across the road in front of me, taking in the endless row of restaurants and hotels lining the street. "Here's what's going to happen. I'm going to park down the street, you're going to give me your room keycard, and you'll wait in the truck."

"But..."

"You want your photo taken?"

She shakes her head and crosses her arms over her chest. "No."

"I'll get your shit and get out. No one knows or cares who I am. You'll be far enough away, no one will see you. No Jo. No photos."

Even though I'm not looking at her, I can feel her eyes on me. "And if he's there?"

"He bigger than me?" I ask her.

"No."

"Is he known for fighting with men instead of women?"

"No."

"You think he'll swing at me?" I ask, not caring if he does because everything she has said about him tells me I can take him with one hand.

She tips her head back and laughs. "I'm pretty sure he'll shit his pants."

I smile and turn my face to glance her way as we sit at a red light less than a mile away from the hotel. "Then we're good. If he's there, I'll grab your shit and he'll stay quiet, and if not, I'll make him quiet."

"And afterward?" she asks.

"We'll head back, and you're free as a bird. Fly away to wherever your heart wants to go."

"It's that simple?"

I furrow my brows, staring at her. "Why wouldn't it be?"

"You don't want anything for helping me?"

"Babe." I shake my head again. "For real?"

"No one does anything without getting something out of it."

"I don't know what shitty people you're around all the time, but I can say for certain, there are, in fact, people who do things only to be nice."

"But you don't know me."

"I have five female cousins who live nearby, and I would hope if they were going through some shit, someone would help them without expecting something in return. My family taught me morals and also that sometimes chicks need a man to help without any questions because it's literally our job to protect the fairer sex."

"Fairer?" She raises an eyebrow. "You mean weaker."

I shake my head, easing off the brake when the traffic starts to move again. "I never said weak. I'm pretty sure the females in my family could kick most guys' asses without even breaking a sweat. You're in need, and I'm here, willing and able to help."

"So, you're going to let me walk away?"

"Jesus. Do you have one decent person in your life?"

"I thought I did."

"You need to find new people," I tell her as I pull into a small ice cream shop next to the hotel. "Give me the keycard," I tell her, ready to get this shit over with.

She reaches into her purse, fishing out the off-white plastic card. "I only want my clothes and makeup. It should all be in my pink suitcase. I didn't unpack before I headed to the pool and Jamison headed to the maid."

"Noted." I take the keycard from her fingers as she holds it out to me, slinking farther down in her seat. "Don't move. I'll be back."

She reaches across the front seat and grabs my wrist, stopping me. "I shouldn't ask you to do this for me. I can go."

I stare at her and then at her hand, where it's latched on to me. "I'm not stopping you from going, but where you go, I go too. Jamison sounded like he's aching for a fight, and if you think you can handle him, you can get that fine ass moving. I'm sure the people waiting to take the photos you keep talking about would love to get those shots."

She blinks, staring at me as she pulls back her hand, settling it in her lap. "No. You go. Get in and get out as quickly as possible."

"If he mouths off..."

"Be careful." She glances down at her fingers, fidgeting. "Jamison is a spiteful man with connections."

I hold back my laughter.

Connections?

We all have connections. Some better than others.

I don't give two shits about Jamison and his people. I really don't give one shit about her either, but I'm not about to let her walk into a potentially dangerous situation to get her things when I have two legs and a hand to grab them.

"Hang tight. Be back in twenty."

"Room 904," she calls out as I slide out of my seat and my feet touch the ground.

"Babe, I'm not old or stupid. You've told me the number five times since we left my place."

"Go," she snaps, waving me away and crossing her feet over each other on the dashboard. "I'll be here."

"Fuckin' pain in my ass," I mutter, shutting the door before hauling my ass toward the hotel on the next block.

The hotel is new and high-class. Nothing like the old run-down motel that stood in its place for decades. The mirrored glass façade is beautiful but looks like it belongs in LA and not Clearwater, Florida.

As I walk into the lobby, I spot a group of people all holding their cameras at the ready exactly as Jo had warned. I stalk right by them without being noticed because they are looking for the girl currently camped out in my truck, instead of me.

Since I am holding the keycard in my hand, no one stops me as I make my way to the elevators and up to the ninth floor. Two quick knocks on the door of Room 904 and no reply before I enter, finding the pink suitcase near the door.

I do a quick sweep, taking in the crazy-ass size of the room. Scratch that. This isn't a room. It is a suite and one of the biggest ones I've ever seen in my life. It drips with wealth and excess. Two things I've never cared much for.

I have my own money. Growing up with a trust fund is something I never felt comfortable with, and I only used the money to buy my house, keeping the rest nestled away for someday when I am too old to work.

As I wrap my fingers around the pink handle, matching the very pink and over-the-top girlie suitcase, a man clears his throat behind me.

"So, she's slumming it," he says. "It's official. She's gone off the deep end."

I turn, the suitcase in one hand, the other curled into a tight fist because I know this is Jamison, and I'll have no problem knocking him on his ass if for nothing else than the way he talked to her.

"Man, I don't know her, and I sure as fuck don't know you. I'm here to get her things and get her on her way. You can either let me pass, not pulling me into your drama or bullshit, or I'm putting you on your ass and still leaving."

He stares at me, puffing himself up like a wild animal trying to look badder than he really is. "You wouldn't hit me," he sneers, tipping up his chin like some rich scumbag who thinks his shit doesn't stink.

"You inviting my fist to that man-made chin?" I ask, taking a step forward.

He steps back.

He's a pretty boy, for sure. Totally Californian with his wavy blond surfer hair and decked out in a dress shirt with the first two buttons undone like he's sexier that way. He's skinny, and I'm pretty damn sure one square, well-placed hit to his jaw and he'd be kissing the carpet.

"I'll sue you," he taunts.

"Ahh, you're a big man," I reply, moving toward him with the pink suitcase, "who hides behind lawyers. Full of talk, but a complete nothing except a complete pussy."

With every step I take toward him, he takes one back. "She's trash, anyway. You can have her."

"Listen, man. She's not mine. I'm not having her. I'm here to get her shit so she can be done with you. She's severing ties. Ending shit. You need to forget her number and pretend she never existed."

He tips that chin again, looking like he's begging me to strike him. "She'll come back. She always does."

It takes everything in me not to pop him for fun. "I heard about your issue." I dip my gaze to his crotch, letting him know I know how small he is.

"Fuck off. I don't have an issue."

"Whatever, man. I got shit to do. You either move out of the doorway, or I move you myself. The carpet could use a new accessory," I say, making my way toward him as he blocks the main hallway.

Before I'm within arm's reach, he steps to the side. "She deserves someone classless like you. Trash begets trash."

I stop, releasing the pink suitcase, and step up to him, backing him into the wall so he has nowhere to go. My face is inches from his, our eyes locked. "I don't know how shit works where you're from, but this is not how shit works here. You talk shit about me, I let that slide. I'm a man. I can take it, especially from someone like you. But when you talk about a woman, one you were supposedly in love with, and call her trash, hurling all kinds of baseless insults at her when she isn't here to defend herself, I'm going to make damn sure it doesn't slide."

"Go ahead." He eggs me on, eyes narrowed, body frozen. "Hit me."

I lurch forward like I'm going to land a shot.

He flinches, screaming like a girl, covering his face.

The laugh that comes out of my mouth echoes through the hallway. What a freaking pansy-ass. I didn't even have to lay a punch for him to almost piss himself.

"Jo's gone, and so am I. But make no mistake, next time, I'm laying you out. Lawyers won't protect you from my fist."

"Redneck," he yells as I walk away, fucking stupid pink suitcase trailing behind me.

"Small-dicked bastard," I reply into the emptiness of the hallway, not even bothering to look back in his direction.

I get more than a few looks as I walk through the hotel lobby with the pink suitcase, but no one says shit to me about it because they know better. Once outside, I retract the handle, carrying the suitcase to make the trip quicker, not wanting any more attention than necessary.

"Lookin' hot, *papi*," some asshole yells out the car window as he sits at the light.

He gets my middle finger but nothing else. My truck and Jo are where I left them. She has her eyes closed, head tipped back, looking like she is waiting for me to bring her an ice cream cone and not her belongings from her weak-ass excuse of a now ex-boyfriend.

Her head tips forward and her eyes pop open as I slide back into the truck cab. "You did it?" she asks, staring at me in disbelief. "He just let you leave?"

"Babe." I gawk at her, wondering what alternate reality she's living in. "He's a weak man. And I'm being kind calling that sorry excuse for a human being part of the male population."

"I used to think he was a good person," she admits.

"You need to find new people if you think he's good. He's a bully and a pussy with the way he throws around his lawyer. No real man says that shit. And no real man cheats on his girl when his girl is as pretty as you are unless he's a shit person too."

"Well...I..." She goes silent, staring at me as I stare at her.

"You're welcome," I tell her, ending the awkward pause. "Let's get you back to your car, and you can be on your way."

"On my way?" she asks, blinking.

"Home or wherever the fuck you're headed."

"I was here for a vacation. I needed an escape."

"Well, Florida's a big state. Lots of places to run away to if you're looking not to be found."

"Yeah," she mutters.

"Ready?"

She nods, not saying anything else as I put the truck in reverse, ready to get out of the city.

"What's wrong?" I ask, seeing her twist her fingers in her lap.

"Nothing," she snaps.

I stop the truck, letting it idle. "Talk to me."

"I don't have anywhere to go. You don't understand."

"Enlighten me."

"Drive, and I'll talk," she tells me, turning toward the

window on her side of the truck, staring at the world passing by.

I finish pulling out, easing into the endless traffic because it's tourist season and the roads to get to the beach are always full. "I'm driving."

"There's nowhere for me to go without being tracked. I know you live a life where you move freely, but I don't. I never have. I'm tracked by my credit cards and social media posts, always followed by photographers or people looking for something from me. Do you know what that's like?"

"Can't say that I do."

"I only need a few days to get my head together before I face the cameras and my family."

I don't know what kind of crazy world she lives in, but it's not anything I've ever experienced or am even remotely familiar with. "So, you're saying you're someone to people?"

"My parents are, and by default, so am I."

"Must suck."

"You have no idea."

"Saw the photographers waiting for you in the hotel."

She turns her head toward me, sadness in her eyes. "They're always waiting for me."

I don't know why I'm about to say what I'm about to say, but I say it anyway. "You need an escape?" I ask her.

"I do. I need to disappear."

"Been twelve hours and they haven't found you yet."

"Nope," she replies. "Not yet."

I sigh, scrubbing my hand quickly across my face. "You can stay at my place for a few days. I have to work so I won't be around much, but you're free to hang out by the pool and relax. I know it's no swanky-ass high-class hotel, but it's private and peaceful." I turn my head toward her, taking in her now-wide eyes.

"You'd let me stay?"

I shrug. "Doesn't matter much to me unless you plan to steal my shit."

"Why would I do that?" she asks, brows drawn down.

"Fuck if I know."

"You're really okay with me staying and invading your space?"

"Again, I gotta work, and it's not like you're hard on the eyes."

"I'm not hard on the eyes?" she asks, hissing the last word.

"Nope. Pretty damn easy to look at, and you're sweet to be around when you're not crying over some weak-ass jagoff who doesn't deserve the tears."

"Are you sure I can stay?"

"Yeah. I don't say shit unless I mean it."

She scoots across the bench seat and places a quick and chaste kiss on my cheek. "Thank you, Nick. You've saved me more than once. I'll pay you back somehow."

I smile, liking the way her lips felt against my skin. "Don't need your money, babe. Don't make a mess of my place, and we're even."

"Can I have the bed?" she asks, and I don't even have to look at her to know she's smiling too.

"Nope."

And just like that, I have a new and very temporary roommate.

Lord help me.

5

JO

Nick drops me off in the driveway with only a few things: his cell phone number programmed into my phone, the key to his house, the address of where he works in case of emergency, and my pink suitcase.

I don't move as he pulls out of the driveway, taking off down the street like he is trying to break a land speed record. I stand in the driveway for about a minute, staring back and forth between the house and the road, and wonder what in the hell happened?

Never in a million years did I think he'd offer for me to stay. Not even when I laid it on pretty thick, telling him I had nowhere else to go to escape the reality that is my life.

After it is clear he isn't coming back, I pull my heavy suitcase through the front door, drop the key on the side table along with my purse, and go right to the couch.

My ass hasn't even hit the cushion when my phone rings.

"Josephine," my mother screeches as soon as I tap the screen.

"Mom," I sigh, bracing myself.

"Where are you? Jamison called and..."

"I'm fine," I answer although she didn't ask me how I was, only where I was.

Naturally, Jamison called her, bending over backward to kiss up to my parents, hoping their success would, somehow, rub off on him.

He isn't unlike the other people in my life. Always looking to get something out of a relationship with me. Something more than my love and friendship, rather status and success, all the while climbing on me and over me to get it.

"Where are you?" she asks again.

"I'm safe."

"That's good, dear, but where?"

"I'm tapping out of reality for a while, Mom. I need a break from everything and everyone in my life. Just know I'm safe, and I've found a little hideaway to find my center again. But don't worry, I'll be back in a week or two."

"Jamison's at the hotel waiting for you to come back. He called in a panic, telling us you're with some crazy ruffian and that he is worried about your safety."

"Of course he did," I mutter, rolling my eyes. "Fuckin' weasel and liar."

"The man threatened him."

"I'm sure he deserved it."

"Josephine," she chides me, sounding completely shocked at my response. "I'm sure the media overstated what happened. Jamison has always been kind and doesn't deserve to have his life threatened by some—"

"Overstated?"

"We know how the paparazzi is. We've dealt with them our entire lives. They always blow everything way out of proportion."

"Mom," I snap, collapsing back on the couch, throwing my arm over my face. "I walked into the room and found Jamison with his face between the legs of the maid."

"Well..." She pauses, clearly clutching those tarnished pearls that hang around her neck, giving her an air of innocence. "Maybe you misinterpreted what was happening?"

"Maybe I misinterpreted what was happening?" I repeat, stupefied.

"You never know. Maybe she needed help with something, and they fell over just as you walked in."

The laughter bubbles out of my throat and right into the receiver of the phone. "Unless something fell into her vagina, Mom, there's no way to misinterpret what I saw. The only thing she needed help with was the orgasm she was clearly in the middle of when I walked in on them."

"Boys will be boys," she hums, clearly dismissing his behavior like she has with my dad more times than I can remember. "If you want to be happy, you have to look the other way instead of trying to find problems."

I bite back the scream that's festering deep in my chest. My mom means well, but she's been a doormat her entire life, settling for shitty relationships and becoming a pro at explaining away bad behavior.

"Do you hear yourself?" I ask her. "You are not normal. The people you surround yourself with are not normal either. I think you forgot about reality, living in your bubble way too long. Boys will be boys is not an acceptable excuse for crappy men who are willing to stick their dick in anything that moves, Mom. I get you're willing to accept mediocrity, but I am not."

"Maybe I should schedule you another appointment with Dr. Jones."

"No." My answer is quick, swift, and leaves no room for error.

There is no way in hell I would go back to a Hollywood psychologist who bought into the same line of thinking as my mother. The same psychologist who tried to modify my way of thinking and behavior so I'd buy into it too.

"We'll talk about setting up an appointment with her when you get home."

"Again, that's a big fat no, Mom."

"We'll see, honey," she says. "And what about the man who threatened Jamison?"

"You mean the man who protected me by getting my things, so I wouldn't have to—"

"Protected you?" she laughs. "I'm sure he didn't do it out of the goodness of his heart. Remember, *boys will be boys*, and nothing is ever for free. He knows who you are, Josephine."

I roll my eyes. "I have to go. My appointment at the spa is in ten minutes," I lie. "I've booked myself every treatment they have over the next week. Until then, I'd prefer to be left alone."

"There's nothing like a good pampering to help one find peace. I'll check in with you in a few days," she replies, glossing right over the fact that I wanted to be left alone for the next seven days.

"Text only. No more voice calls. I'm going to try the technique Dr. Jones taught me about silence and centering."

"Oh yes. That's always helpful. I'll text you in a few days," she amends her last statement.

The technique is total bullshit. Something I made up when I didn't want to talk to my mother, which has been more often than not over the last few years.

I can never do anything right in her eyes. My relationship failures are always my fault, never the man's.

I am the wild child who needs taming in her eyes, instead of the doting daughter of Hollywood elite.

"Got to run."

"Bye, dear," she says before the line goes dead and the room is filled with nothing but silence.

"Fucking bananas," I mutter, staring up at the white ceiling. "Not one normal person in my life."

The closest person I have to normal is my best friend, but her parents are bigger Hollywood movie stars than mine, and I haven't seen her in three years. My father is more normal than my mother but spends more time away, chasing tail on movie sets all over the world. My parents haven't gotten along in well over ten years, but instead of getting divorced, they've decided to lead separate lives to save face in front of the press.

That's the life I grew up in.

Dysfunctional is an understatement.

I was raised by my nanny, a sweet woman who had more sense than everyone else in my life put together. She'd spend hours reading to me, opening my eyes to things outside my entitled little bubble...much to my mother's dismay.

I push myself up, glancing around the living room. My pink suitcase sticks out like a sore thumb against the copious amounts of black and white.

"What am I doing here?" I ask no one but myself. "And who is this guy?"

The house does not match the man. When he pulled up next to my car, sitting on his motorcycle, I never suspected he'd live in a place as well put-together and impressive as this.

My phone rings next to me, and I glance down, seeing Kimberly's name flash across the screen. "Hey," I say, answering her call because usually, she's somewhat normal to talk to, unlike my parents.

"Babe," she replies and breaks out into a fit of giggles.

"Hardy har har." I pause, waiting for her to get in her laughs at my expense.

She clears her throat. "Sorry. I couldn't stop myself."

"I just got off the phone with my mother."

The sound of her sucking in a breath between her teeth is unmistakable. "And how did that go?"

"Oh, you know...a dash of insanity mixed with over-dramatics." I rise to my feet, not able to sit any longer.

If I am going to spend the next however long talking to Kimberly, I'll at least use the time to check out the rest of the house since I've only seen the kitchen, living room, and bathroom.

"Your mother will never change, Jo. She lives for the drama, and her crazy comes naturally."

"I know," I tell her, walking down the hallway, pushing open the first door after the bathroom. My gaze sweeps around the space, not feeling guilty for invading his privacy. "She pisses me off."

"That is your one constant in life."

"Yeah," I mutter, hesitantly stepping inside what I can only assume is his bedroom.

"Are you okay? Are you safe?" Kimberly asks. "When are you coming back?"

"I'm fine and, yes, of course I'm safe," I reply, pressing my finger against the black comforter neatly laid out across his king-sized bed. "I don't know when I'm coming back. I need a reset."

"Did you find a new hotel?"

"No. I'm at his place."

"Wait," she says, papers rustling in the background. "You're still there?"

I explain the situation, how Nick went to the hotel and then invited me to stay on the way back, and how I said yes without hesitation. I tell her all this as I crawl on top of his bed, stretching out and letting my body melt into the softness, and somehow, unlike her normal self, Kimberly stays quiet and lets me ramble.

"He sounds so, so..."

"Yeah," I whisper.

"You don't even know what I was going to say."

"Yes, I do."

"No. You don't. Maybe I was going to say he sounds like an ax murderer."

"Liar," I mumble as my eyes begin to grow heavy, exhaustion from the last twenty-four hours starting to take hold. "You were going to say he sounds dreamy."

She chuckles. "You know I don't like these Hollywood pretty boys. I prefer my men to be more...manly. Chop me some wood or fix my flat tire kind of guys."

This isn't news to me. Kimberly went out of her way to find men who didn't fall into either the bohemian way of life in California or who were part of the Hollywood establishment.

"Is he hot? His driver's license photo was blurry because you're a shit photographer."

"Shut up. My hands were shaking, and he's sure as hell not hard on the eyes."

"Send me a photo," she tells me as I yawn. "Shirtless preferred."

"How am I supposed to do that?"

"I don't know, but make it happen."

"He's not the selfie type of guy."

"Girl, you're ticking my boxes."

I place the phone next to my head and curl onto my side, flattening out one leg and curling the other toward my chest. "His house is unusually clean."

"Maybe he has a housekeeper."

Now it's my turn to chuckle. "He is not the housekeeper type."

"All kinds of people have housekeepers or maids who come to clean their house."

"If this guy has a housekeeper, I'll buy you a new pair of your favorite red-bottomed shoes."

"Now you're speaking my language. Well, I hate to cut this short, but I have a conference call in a few minutes."

"It's fine. I think I'm going to close my eyes for a couple minutes anyway."

"Promise me you're okay."

"I promise. I've never felt more certain about things. I'm right where I want to be, and no one knows where I am, which couldn't make me happier."

"Text me later after the hottie comes home. Keep me updated and get the damn picture. Bye," she says, lingering on the last word for a few seconds.

"Bye, Kimberly," I say, watching the screen go black before closing my eyes.

The bed dips, and my eyes fly open.

"Comfy?" Nick asks, sitting next to me, staring down at me.

I scramble to a sitting position, my eyes blurry from sleep and my heart racing. "What time is it?"

"Six."

"Six?" I widen my eyes, my sleepiness suddenly gone. "I slept for six hours?"

He shrugs. "Don't know, babe. I got here and found you lying in my bed, curled in a ball."

I look around, forgetting I'd crawled onto his bed, a bed I wasn't invited into but made myself at home in, nonetheless. "I'm sorry," I say, moving toward the edge.

He grabs my wrist, stopping me before I have a chance to scramble to my feet. "Stop," he says gently, and I freeze.

I turn my head to see his face. His eyes are soft, a smile playing on his lips, and looking nowhere near upset. "I didn't mean to fall asleep, and I never should've come into your room."

"When you're tired, you're tired. The only cure for that is some shut-eye. And since my room has the only bed and it's the most comfortable thing in the world, I don't blame you for crawling on top and getting some rest."

I stare at him. "You're not mad?"

"If a man finds you in his bed and he's mad about it,

he needs to get his head examined and his manhood checked."

I blink, gawking at him. "Um…" I mumble, sounding like an incoherent idiot.

"Anyway, I came home early to see if you wanted to go out with us. Some of my buddies are headed to the bar for a few beers."

"How fancy do I need to get for these beers?"

"There's no dress code, babe. You can go like that."

I peer down, taking in my wrinkled clothing. There's no way I am going out in public like this, let alone meeting any of his friends. "Can I have ten minutes?"

"I need a shower. Grease," he says, and I let my gaze travel down his body, lingering on his chest, which is indeed covered by a white tank top and splotches of black grease.

I gulp, trying not to choke on my tongue at the way his muscles are more pronounced thanks to the tight, bright material. "A shower would be nice," I breathe.

His smile widens. "On your own or with me?"

I blink again. "My own," I snap, not trusting myself in the shower with him. There's also the fact that I don't really know him, although I've slept all night on his couch and now in his bed.

He laughs. "You can shower first," he tells me, tipping his head toward the bathroom behind him that's attached to his bedroom. "Use mine. It's nicer than the guest one."

"I don't know. I've already overstepped my welcome."

He shakes his head again. "I don't want an argument. There're fresh towels and everything you need in there. I'm going to go make a sandwich while you shower, and then it's my turn. Save me a little hot water, okay?"

I nod, blinking like a mute idiot.

"I'll use the guest bathroom, and you can get ready in here."

"Okay." I find his selflessness unnerving and oddly refreshing.

"Jeans and a T, babe."

"What?"

"Wear jeans and a T. None of the over-the-top shit you no doubt have packed in that pretty pink suitcase."

I scrunch my nose. "Who says I have fancy shit?"

He barks out a laugh as he stands, the bed righting itself with the loss of his weight. "You're funny. Thirty minutes," he calls out as he makes his way toward the open bedroom door. "I'll put your suitcase in here for when you're finished."

"Um, thanks," I say, but it comes out sounding more like a question than an honest reply.

And with that, he's gone.

I sit on his bed, staring at the open door and empty bedroom. "What the fuck?"

"Thirty minutes," he yells out like he heard me or my inability to move. "Starting now."

I scramble to my feet, running toward his bathroom and sealing myself inside. Plastering my back against the door, I'm momentarily stunned by the gray-and-white marble and floor-to-ceiling shower encased in glass, looking like it was built more for a party than a single man.

"Holy shit," I say softly as I push away from the wooden door, moving toward the shower that's calling my name.

Maybe, just maybe, this isn't the worst idea in the world.

6

JO

Nick lied.

The *buddies* weren't *buddies* at all.

"These are my cousins—Mammoth, Tamara, Pike, Gigi, Jett, and Lily." He points at each person as he rattles off their names. "This is Jo."

"Hi," I reply, trying to keep calm as my stomach twists, but I still plaster on a smile. "Nice to meet you."

Six sets of eyes are on me, studying me with curiosity as I stand next to Nick, his hand lightly pressing against the small of my back. The heat of his palm seeps through my thin T-shirt, and I hate to admit it, but I like the feel of his hand on me.

The second girl he gestured to leans forward, narrowing her eyes. "Have we met before?" she asks.

"Nope. I don't think so. I'm not from around here." I keep the smile on my face, praying she won't recognize me.

"Nicky, when you said you rescued a girl in a parking lot, I never expected her to look like this."

I swing my gaze his way, glaring at him. "You did not rescue me from a parking lot."

He smirks. "Technically, I did."

"I was trying to grab a few hours of sleep before I could drive, but you stopped and badgered me until I said I'd come home with you."

"Badgered?" He laughs, putting a little more pressure on the small of my back with his hand. "Babe, be real."

One of the women motions toward the two empty seats with a shit-eating grin on her face. "Sit down. We have a lot to discuss."

I quickly slide into one of the open seats, needing to get away from his touch because I like it too much. Nick plops down next to me but moves his chair closer so our thighs are almost touching.

"Now, I'm Tamara. The best cousin," a woman with dark hair, hazel-green eyes, and a vibrant pink tube top says. She's holding a bottle of beer in one hand, elbow propped on the table, and sitting forward with her gaze firmly planted on me. "Do I know you from somewhere?"

"She's from Cali," Nick answers for me.

Tamara's eyes flicker to him. "Let her talk."

He lifts his hands but stays quiet.

"Cali?" she asks.

I nod.

"You want a beer?" he asks me, motioning toward the waitress.

I nod again, and he holds up two fingers to the woman as she heads our way and then spins on her heel.

"Whereabouts in Cali?" Tamara asks.

The man next to her, his body covered in tattoos on every patch of visible skin except his face, lifts her like she weighs nothing and drops her in his lap. "Princess, maybe she doesn't feel like being grilled."

She turns her head, smiling at whom I can only assume is her man. "Sparky, I'm not grilling. This is called talking, something I know you guys don't always seem to do so well in crowds."

"Hi," another woman says. "I'm Gigi, the oldest cousin. Ignore them all. You don't have to answer any questions. Tonight is about getting out of the house and unwinding."

"Thanks," I say softly, twisting my fingers in my lap.

Gigi winks at me and then turns her attention toward Mammoth and Tamara. "How was work today?"

"Same shit, different day," Tamara answers. "The guys finished up a car that's been in the shop for the last two months. I'll be happy to see it off the books."

"Is that the kick-ass Chevelle?"

"Yep," the tattooed guy replies with one arm holding his girl and his hand resting against her stomach. "It's sweet as fuck now too."

"There's something bittersweet about finishing a project and having to start on something else," Nick says as the waitress returns with two beers.

"Hey, Nicky," she purrs. "Haven't seen you in a

while. Missed you around here." As she places the beers on the table, she leans forward, putting her tits right in his face.

He doesn't seem fazed and does nothing to move out of their orbit. "Been busy, Corinne," he says dismissively.

"You shouldn't work so hard." She doesn't move back and sure as hell doesn't move her giant tits out of his face. "If you need to relax—"

"Relaxin' now," he cuts her off. "Hanging with my family and my girl." He ticks his head toward me. "So, while I appreciate the offer, it's a no."

My girl. My mouth opens and closes as my eyes widen. Unless I'm hearing things, he called me his girl, and to say I'm shocked is an understatement.

She raises her hand and twists a finger around a lock of his hair that's fallen against his forehead. "When you get done playing with girls, you know where to find a real woman," she says, grinning down at him, almost salivating.

"Noted," he mutters.

The man next to Gigi, with a heavy beard and colorful ink covering his arms, clears his throat. "We could take another round, 'Rin."

Her gaze flickers to him, but her tits are *still* in Nick's face. "Coming right up, Pike." She winks his way before sauntering off.

"I hate that triflin' bitch," Gigi mutters. "I really want to pop her in the tits and then her face."

"Darlin'," the man next to her says, lifting her hand to

his lips, kissing her fingers. "No fighting. She's not worth it."

"My hormones make me ragey, and she's a thirsty bitch for the way she talks to all the guys even while y'all are sitting next to us."

The other woman at the table laughs. "Girl, you know the hormones are ridiculous when you're preggers, and yes, she's extremely thirsty."

"Thirsty?" I ask, confused. "And wait, so if you're all cousins, then..."

The woman laughs. "We girls are Nicky's blood cousins, and the men are our husbands—which, by default and legally, makes them his cousins too."

"Phew," I mumble, laughing softly. "That would've been awkward otherwise."

"We're in the Deep South, Jo, but we're not backward. My guy, Mammoth," Tamara says, running her fingernails across his arm that's around her middle, "was in an MC, and he and Pike go way back."

"MC?" I ask.

"Motorcycle club."

I swallow, letting my gaze rake over the men for far too long, but not out of lust.

"Anyway," she sighs, continuing without making a comment about how I'm staring a little too much, "they're not anymore. Want to know more?"

Nick pushes the beer in front of me. "You're going to need this because nothing Tamara does is quick, especially talking."

"Fucker," she mutters, narrowing her eyes.

"I'll tell her," Gigi offers. "Lily and Tamara can talk for hours, giving you a headache like you never knew existed. Pike and Mammoth were in an MC but aren't anymore, as she said. Mammoth, Tamara, and Nick work at an auto body shop together, but they also own it. Pike, Lily, and I work together at our family's tattoo parlor, and Jett works for our uncles at their security company. I'm married to Pike, Tamara's married to Mammoth, and Lily is married to Jett. We're only four out of the eleven cousins in our family, but we're the oldest and best."

Tamara laughs. "I'm pretty sure Mello and Rocco would disagree."

"Those two little bastards disagree with everything," Lily rolls her eyes. "The older they get, the more trouble they become."

"They're boys, baby. That's what we do," her man, Jett, says as he slides his arm around the back of her chair, resting his hand on her shoulder.

"So, what do you do, Jo?" Tamara asks, moving back to me, making my head spin.

I lift the beer to my lips, taking a sip while I try to figure out a good way to answer the question. All eyes at the table are still on me except Nick's.

"You don't have to answer any questions," he tells me as I guzzle the beer like I'm a professional drinker.

"I work in PR," I tell them as soon as I stop drinking and come up for air.

"Really?" Tamara gasps.

"Yeah." I smile, lying like it's second nature.

And it almost is, especially with parents like mine. They wouldn't know the truth if it smacked them in the face and left a mark.

Tamara perks up, resting her chin on her hand. "I have a degree in marketing. It's what I do at the garage. Which firm? Maybe I've heard of it."

I shake my head, turning the bottle in my hands, trying not to make it completely obvious that I'm fumbling for an answer. "It's a small boutique house in LA, serving only a few select clients."

"Do you work with celebrities?" Her eyes get wide. "You have to tell me who."

"One or two, maybe." I smile nervously. "But we have strict NDAs."

"NDA?" she asks, blinking.

"Nondisclosure agreements."

"Damn," she hisses. "That sucks."

"Yeah," I mutter, nodding slowly. "Totally."

"Are we done with the third degree?" Nick asks, staring down his cousins.

Gigi peers over the rim of her drink. "It's called small talk, Nicky. You should try it sometime."

I let out a giggle at his nickname and the fact that they're quick to put him in his place. And when Nick's eyes swing my way, I slap my hand across my mouth, trying to stifle the sound.

"Something funny?"

I shake my head, holding my hand against my mouth

to stop myself from laughing louder.

He stares at me for a moment, our eyes locked. His face is serious while mine is contorted as I try to fight off the giggle, but the look on his face only makes it harder.

"Let me show you how small talk works," Gigi tells him and turns her gaze toward her cousin Tamara. "How was work today?"

"Uneventful. Finished a car. Worked on some ads."

Her husband kisses her temple. "Don't let her fool you. She started a massive ad campaign that already has the phone ringing off the hook."

"Thanks, Sparky." She smiles, melting into his touch.

"Big deal," Lily, the quieter of the three cousins, announces. "I pierced ten peens this week and so many nips, I lost count."

"Peens and nips?" I ask.

"Cocks and tits," Tamara answers. "Lily isn't into ink like Gigi and Pike, but she is one of the best damn body piercers in the area."

"Dayum. That has to be painful."

"Which one?" Lily asks me.

I shrug. "Both sound awful."

"I don't know," she replies. "All the guys at the table have their peens pierced, and the girls...well, I'm the only one with my nipples still how they were when I was born."

I turn my head, swinging my gaze to Nick, and blush. Based on what she said, Nick has his *peen* pierced too.

"I know you're thinking about my cock now, babe. Can see it in your eyes." Nick smirks.

"I am not," I shoot back, lying my ass off because I am, in fact, thinking about his dick.

He raises an eyebrow, staring down at me with those haunting blue eyes.

"Okay. Okay. Maybe a little, but more about the piercing than your actual manhood." I smile, feeling proud of myself and my answer, even if the words aren't true.

"Lily," Gigi pipes up, leaning back in her chair. "Your nipples are far from how they were when you were born. Breastfeeding has massacred them."

"No, it didn't," Lily argues, bringing her hands up to cup her breasts. "I mean, they're still there, and they're not that bad."

"I've seen them," Tamara tells the table. "They're almost normal."

"You're an asshole," Lily snaps.

Tamara smiles. "Sweetie, be proud of those things. You can almost poke an eye out with them. If I've ever seen a set of nipples that should be pierced, it's yours. You should think about doing it."

"I know, but..." Her voice trails off. "I can't pierce myself, and who the hell else am I going to ask to do them for me? My dad?" Her eyes widen. "That wouldn't be horrifying or anything."

I laugh again, this time quieter and behind the safety of my beer bottle. I love how open they are with one another.

How real they are with one another. Something I don't experience much with the people in my life back in California.

I also like that they don't seem to know who I am, and if they do, they don't care. It's nice to be a normal person, blending in with those around me instead of sticking out like a sore thumb.

"I can do them," Pike, Gigi's man, offers, and all eyes turn on him as the table quiets. "What?"

"You'd pierce her nipples?" Gigi asks, blinking at him like someone's poked her in her eye.

"Well, I mean..." He smiles. "No one else in the shop has piercing experience except me. You going to do it?" he asks her.

Gigi's lips twist, but she holds his gaze. "I'd do an awful job. They'd probably be lopsided or some shit. So, the answer is no, but I can't believe how quickly you offered your services."

"Darlin', they're nipples, and it's work."

"I don't know how I feel about you seeing my wife's breasts," Jett tells Pike.

The conversation is so refreshing. Any other people in the world and we'd be talking about my life, my parents' lives, or celebrities. But not with this group. They're busy discussing nipples and penises like they're talking about the weather and if it'll rain next week.

Pike cocks his head, staring down Jett. "Do you want her dad to do it? 'Cause I'm sure that would be a lovely conversation to have with Mike about how you want his daughter to pierce her nipples to help heighten her pleasure during sex."

"Oh Jesus," Lily mumbles, covering her face with her palms. "Can we stop talking about my breasts?"

"No," Tamara laughs.

Nick leans over, bringing his mouth so close to my ear, I can feel his warm breath against my skin. "I'm sorry about this."

I turn my face, our lips close enough I could kiss him. "Why?" I ask, soaking in the blueness of his eyes, almost losing myself in their depths. "I'm having a good time. They're really great. You're lucky to have such a close relationship with them."

He stares back at me, his eyes roaming my face but otherwise unreadable. "As long as they're not making you uncomfortable."

"Not at all, but I could use another drink."

"Another beer?" he asks.

"No." I stare into his eyes from only a few inches away. "Something harder."

I don't need to pull back to know there's a smile on his face. "You want hard, babe, I got you covered."

Fuck.

My mind instantly goes to his dick and the fact that it's pierced. I wonder what kind, how big, and what it looks like. All questions I'll never have answered and never had in my mind until a few minutes ago.

Nick lifts his hand, motioning over the thirsty waitress again. She's quick too, almost tripping over a few people as she runs toward the table.

"Hey," she wheezes.

"A round of Jäger for the entire table."

"Oh lord. It's going to be one of those nights," one of the cousins mutters, but I'm too busy gawking at Nick.

The waitress smiles down at him, leaning too far into his personal space. A few more inches and her tits would be right in his face again. "Can I get you anything else?"

Without hesitation and like he's done it a million times before, Nick slides his arm around me, resting his hand on my shoulder. "We're good."

I smile, leaning into him, plastering myself against his hard body. "Yeah, we're good," I repeat, sounding like a complete moron.

The woman gives me a sour look before she stalks away, not as happy as she was when she arrived.

"Do you have any piercings?" one of the cousins asks me, but I'm too busy staring at Nick and loving the way his body feels against mine to even notice.

"What?" I ask, blinking away the fog of lust, and turn my attention back toward the rest of the table. "Were you talking to me or her?"

Gigi swipes her hand through the air in the direction the big-breasted bimbo walked away. "Not her. You, silly. Do you have any piercings or tattoos?"

I suddenly feel out of place. "No."

Tamara gawks at me. "Not even a small tattoo hidden somewhere on your body?"

I shake my head.

"We should fix that," she tells me. "Something small and meaningful."

"I don't know," I say, my voice wavering.

"Think about it. Gigi and Pike are some of the best tattoo artists in the state," she replies. "I'd hate for you to leave without something to remember your trip by."

"There are less painful souvenirs," Mammoth states the obvious. "Tattoos aren't something to jump into without thought."

Tamara lifts her hand to his face, running her fingers over his beard. "Sparky, you're covered in tats. I don't think one little quarter-sized tattoo on her body will be life-altering. She could put it on her back even, and then she'll never have to see it again. It'll be there, imprinted on her skin like ink in a book, telling part of her life's story."

"You make it sound so beautiful," Lily says. "You should really work on an ad campaign for the shop."

"We don't need more business," Gigi tells Lily, shaking her head. "We're already booked three months out, for fuck's sake."

"You can never have too much business," Mammoth tells Gigi, pointing his index finger at her while the rest of his fingers are wrapped around a beer bottle. "It's better to have a wait list than no list at all."

"We have a very, very, very long wait list."

"Here we go," Thirsty Corinne sings, placing the tray of shots on the table. She sets everyone's down gingerly,

Pike taking Gigi's, until she gets to me, and then she slams the sucker down so hard, half of mine splashes out onto the table. "Enjoy." And with that, she's gone.

"Think she finally realized she isn't getting any Nicky dick anytime soon?" Gigi teases, laughing hysterically.

"I fuckin' hope so," Nick mutters.

"You said Nicky dick," Lily repeats, giggling. "That sounded so..."

"Childish?" Gigi asks, finishing the statement.

"I don't know. It was quite original," Pike tells her, earning him two middle fingers and a playful smile.

He reaches over, hauling her onto his lap. His arms tighten around her, and she wiggles against his legs, laughing. "Is that a promise, darlin'?" he asks quietly against her ear, but loud enough for everyone at the table to hear.

There are a few things I know in this moment.

One.

I really like these people. Everything about them is fun and easy. The love is evident. I instantly wish I had cousins to sit around with and laugh, teasing one another over stupid shit.

Two.

I've missed out on a lot in life. My parents are shit, and their families are even bigger shit. After my parents hit it big in Hollywood, they immediately distanced themselves from their families. They felt the move was justified, but I was the one who ultimately paid the price.

Three.

Nick may have talked in partial sentences and come off like a smug, arrogant asshole, but he is more. His family loves him, and he is funny, sexy, and can flirt without putting in much effort.

Four.

If I stick around too long, leaving will be impossible.

7

NICK

"Nicky," she slurs, pawing at the buckle on my jeans as I set her on my bed. "Lemme shee it."

I grab her hands, moving them away from my dick, hanging on by a thread here. "Someone had too much Jäger."

"It was so good, though," she laments, smiling so big, her eyes close.

"You won't be saying that in the morning, babe."

"You know..." She collapses backward, closing her eyes as her head hits the mattress. "I used to hate when you called me babe, but now..." She stops talking, and I think she's passed out. I back away, but her leg comes out, hooking her heel around my calf like she has drunk superpowers. "Now, I like it."

I bend over, grabbing her foot and prying it loose from my body. "That's good, babe. Whatever makes you happy."

"You want to make me happy? Show me your *peen*." She instantly giggles, rolling to her side and trying to push herself up but failing.

I shake my head, staring down at her. "That's a hard no."

"Nicky," she mumbles, doing everything she can to make her eyes open wider and looking absolutely ridiculous. "Don't say hard when talking about your peen."

"Don't talk about my dick by calling it a peen."

She giggles again, totally drunk and freaking adorable as fuck. "Fine. Show me your dick."

"It's still a no, babe."

She moves like a ninja and has her hands at my belt buckle again. "Come on. A little peek."

I grab her wrists, stopping her. "Tomorrow."

She tips her head back, staring at me with eyes that aren't focusing. "You promise?"

"I do," I lie. "You can see it all you want tomorrow."

Damn it.

There's nothing in the world I'd love to do more than show her my cock, but not while she's drunk. I don't want to be anyone's regret, and I sure as hell don't bang chicks so fucked up, they won't have any memories of the experience the next day.

She gives me a lopsided smile, no longer struggling to break her hands free of my hold. "As long as you promise."

"I do."

She leans back, trying to take me with her, but I let

go, and she falls back. "Can I ask one more thing?" she asks, stretching against my mattress, looking perfect in my bed.

"Sure, babe. Anything."

"Will you lie with me tonight? I'm lonely."

I glance up, cursing the fucking universe for putting me in this situation, but I have no one to blame except myself. I was the rocket scientist who offered her a place to stay. I could've and probably should've sent her on her way after I picked up her suitcase at the hotel, but something about it didn't feel right.

"Please," she begs, running her hand along the mattress next to her. "I won't try anything. I promise."

I can't stop the smile from spreading across my face. She's so drunk, she has no idea how much I want to crawl in the bed and fuck her for hours. It's no hardship being around her. She's beautiful, thoughtful, and although some parts of her life might be a mess, she's not a complete disaster. I can't say that about most of the chicks who end up under me.

I rub the back of my neck as she wiggles her fingers, still silently pleading with me to join her.

"Come on. I'll behave," she promises. "Hold me for one night, and I'll never ask for anything again."

"It's not a good idea."

"Jamison never held me," she confesses. "No one has in years."

"Fuck," I mutter, toeing off my boots before yanking my T-shirt over my head.

She tips her head, staring at my body. "God, you're so pretty."

"No more talking," I tell her as I slide into the bed next to her.

She curls into me instantly, resting her head on my shoulder. "No more talking," she repeats.

I turn my head as I snake my arm around her back, finding a bare patch of skin to rest my hand on. "Night, babe."

"Night, Nicky."

"Sweet dreams," I reply to her.

She nuzzles harder against my side, tilting her head to look at me. "I hope they're dreams of you."

My stomach twists and turns before knotting. "Eyes, babe."

She blinks, batting her eyelashes, still not focusing on my face.

"Close 'em," I tell her, holding her tighter.

Her eyes flutter closed, and she sighs, sounding content in my arms. She feels like she belongs there, which, to me, is more than troubling.

I bury my face in the pile of blond hair and inhale the scent of lavender, something I get a whiff of every time she comes near me.

She lifts her leg, throwing it over mine. "So warm," she breathes.

"Sleep," I repeat, and a few moments later, she's out.

I'm not far behind as I stare at the ceiling, wondering how I was stupid enough to put myself in this kind of situation. One where I am falling a little bit for a woman I've only known for twenty-four hours.

I know nothing about her, but none of that seems to matter.

The only thing I know for sure is that she feels like she was made to sleep in my arms every night. And I'm not sure I'll ever be able to sleep without her there again.

Hot. All I can feel is overwhelming heat, almost suffocating me. My eyes snap open, and the weight hits me next, followed by another wave of warmth.

I tip my head down, finding Jo's body on top of me, her head nestled in my chest, her arms at my sides, hands holding my arms. Her legs are caged in mine and her middle is resting against my very hard morning wood.

Shit.

I suck in a breath, staring back up at the ceiling, and slide my hands under her armpits, trying to move her off me and praying she doesn't wake up.

"No," her small voice objects, groggy with sleep, and I freeze. "Don't move."

"I'm hot, babe."

"Yes, yes, you are." She tightens her hold, locking my body under hers. "But if you move right now, I think I'll lose everything in my stomach."

"You need some water."

"I need stillness," she begs and then groans, smashing her face into my bare chest. "And quiet."

"Babe." I move my hands to her back, rubbing small circles against the skin at the top of her bra she somehow stripped down to while I was sleeping. "We can't stay like this forever. You need water and nourishment."

She grips my biceps harder. "I need five more minutes before I attempt to move."

"Five minutes," I mutter, keeping the circles going, hoping to stave off her throwing up the remains of last night all over me and my bed.

I slept like a rock. I didn't feel her get out of bed to toss her shirt to the side, and I didn't feel her climbing on top of me, attaching her body to mine like she was one of those finger monkey toys Lily's daughter seems to love so much.

I can't remember a time I slept so well.

Another thing that is concerning, besides the fact that I like her lying this way against me even more than I liked her smashed against my body last night.

"How do people do this all the time?"

"Snuggle?" I ask her.

She lifts her head, drool running out of the corner of her mouth, her mascara smudged. "Get shit-faced. How do people do it all the time and function?" she asks before she drops her head back to my chest, clearly not ready to move.

"They get used to it somehow. They build up a tolerance, and when that doesn't work, they drink a little hair of the dog."

"Hair of the what?" she asks against my skin, the puddle of drool between us moving with her lips.

"They have something to drink to chase away the shit feeling."

"Oh Jesus. Who could drink when they feel this shitty?"

"I can make you a Bloody Mary."

She moves her hand, flopping it against my face, feeling across my skin until she finds my lips. She presses her fingers against my mouth, holding it shut. "Don't talk," she tells me. "No talk of alcohol or anything. I still have four minutes."

"This is kind of—"

"Shh." She presses her fingers down harder, trying to stop me from saying anything else.

But somehow, I get out an, "Okay," before she places her entire palm against the lower half of my face. I don't argue with her on how much time she has left, clearly more than a minute elapsing from the moment she made me promise to give her five.

"How many shots did I have?"

"Six," I mutter against her palm.

"Fuck," she hisses, releasing my lips and lifting up on her elbows, squinting down at me. "You let me drink that much?"

I move my hands, holding her sides, careful not to touch her breasts or even let my gaze dip down to them.

"Let you?" I ask, staring straight in her eyes and avoiding her breasts even if it kills me. And it sure as fuck does because I want to see her...all of her.

"You should've told me to stop after three."

I laugh. "Babe, I tried. You told me, and I quote, 'I'm a grown-ass woman, and no one tells me what to do, especially you.' So what the hell was I supposed to do?"

She blinks, but her eyes don't close at the same time, totally out of sync and probably still a little fucked up. "You could've taken me home instead of letting me drink more."

"Tried that too, babe."

She wrinkles her nose. "Is that me?"

"Is what you?" I furrow my brows, wondering if she's still totally obliterated.

"That smell." She grimaces.

My face softens. "The alcohol?"

"Yeah." She nods, her eyes widening as she clamps her mouth shut and starts to move off me.

I lift up, resting on my elbows, watching her take off, moving faster than I've ever seen her move before. She disappears a second later, slamming my bathroom door shut before the sound of her heaving fills the room.

I roll out of bed, knowing she won't be back anytime soon, and even if she is, I don't really want any part of her until she showers and brushes her teeth. I, as a man, have my limits, and puke is it.

Stalking toward the kitchen, I can still hear her from the hallway, emptying her stomach and probably filled with complete and utter regret. I grab a cup and two pills before making my way back toward the bedroom.

Knocking, I whisper, "Jo."

Nothing but a groan comes as a response.

"You okay?"

"Oh God," she mutters. "I think I'm dying."

"I'm coming in," I announce before touching the handle.

"No. Don't," she snaps, her voice echoing off the sides of the toilet bowl. "I don't want you to see me this way."

"You're fine," I tell her, figuring I've seen enough drunk chicks in my life, what's another one. But dear God, I am wrong.

When I open the door, she has her face planted in the toilet bowl, her hair a few inches in the water and her legs on the floor, stretched out, with her body contorted in a way I didn't think was humanly possible.

I crouch down next to her, pulling her hair back with one hand, not caring about the puke toilet water that is now trickling down my fingers and her back. "I need you to drink some water, babe."

"I need to die," she mumbles, turning her head and resting her chin against the toilet seat. "Let me go."

"Come on." I lift up the cup, still holding her hair with the other hand. "You'll feel better."

Her eyes widen again, and she bends her head back into the bowl, emptying her stomach even more. I don't know how she has anything left after all these hours and the sounds she was making when I made my way to the kitchen and back.

"You're going to be okay," I promise, waiting for her to finish.

"No. I'm not," she groans into the bowl.

She curls her arms tighter around the seat, closing off my ability to see her face and the puke. I release her hair, resting it against her back, and set down the cup, trying to ignore the vomit coating my hands.

Turning on the shower, I wash my hands, getting rid of the remnants from last night and making sure the water is the perfect temperature. She needs to drink something, take the pills, and wash herself off before curling back into bed to sleep off whatever is left in her system.

A small whimper comes from the toilet and then a groan of agony.

"Come on, babe. You need to shower and right yourself."

"Right myself?" She turns her head to see me. "I'd like to know how to make that happen quickly."

"Drink, pills, sleep. It's the only thing that'll help."

I pull her back, kneeling behind her, taking her weight. "I brought you water," I tell her, reaching for the cup on the counter and handing it to her before grabbing the two pills. "Drink it and take those."

She doesn't argue as she relaxes back into me, puke now on my chest. Nothing with this chick has been easy since the moment she walked into my life. Part of it is her fault, but getting her drunk and letting her get shit-faced is completely and absolutely mine.

"Good girl," I say, taking the cup from her hands when she polishes off the entire contents. "Sit still for a minute and make sure it stays down and then a quick shower."

"What about you?" she asks.

"What about me?"

"You're covered in my puke."

I glance down, wincing. "I'll survive. Had worse shit on me in my life."

She tips her head back, gawking at me. "Like what?"

"I don't want to talk about it."

"Liar," she teases, but she doesn't smile.

"I'll shower after you once you're back in bed."

"You could take one with me..."

I shake my head. "That wouldn't be good for either of us."

She twists her lips. "It's not like I've never seen a naked man before, Nicky."

"Babe." I smile. "You've seen boys, but I am a man. And once you see all of me, you'll never be happy with anything else."

She rolls her eyes and instantly lifts her arms, grabbing her head. "Fuck. The headache."

"Sit in the shower for a while. It'll help relax you. Don't try standing," I tell her.

"Can you take off my pants for me? I don't think I have the energy."

I stare at her, studying her face, knowing this is a fucked-up request but understanding the necessity of help, especially in the state she's in. I nod, moving my hands to her jeans and working the button before pulling down the zipper. "Lift up," I tell her, and she does, raising her ass up far enough off the tile for me to yank off her jeans and throw them toward the door. "The rest you do yourself."

"Is Nicky shy?"

"No," I correct her. "Nicky's horny and has a smokin'-hot still-drunk chick half naked, along with morning wood still rearing its ugly head."

"Oh," she gasps.

"In ya go, babe," I say as I lift her by her ass and deposit her behind me in the shower spray. "Come out when you're done."

She gives me a sad smile as the water beats down on her, but then she closes her eyes, relaxing back into the tile wall. "Thank you," she whispers as I close the door, sealing the steam inside.

I don't watch. I don't stick around. I haul ass out of the room and curse myself the entire time for the clusterfuck I've created and the wreckage I have no doubt she'll leave behind in her wake.

8

JO

I TIPTOE OUT OF THE BEDROOM, MY TEETH BRUSHED, hair pulled back, a fresh change of clothes, and feeling a little more human than I did earlier.

Nick's eyes are on me the moment I step foot out into the hallway. "Feel better?" he asks, his blue eyes studying me.

"Yeah." I pull at the cuffs of my oversized sweatshirt I brought in case I needed it. "Thank you for being so kind."

"Babe, we all need help at some point, and what kind of person wouldn't help?"

I shrug. Jamison wouldn't have helped. I know that from experience. If I was sick, he'd do everything short of putting on a hazmat suit before coming anywhere near me. "What are you reading?" I ask, changing the subject.

"*Hot Rod.*" He lifts the magazine, showing me the front with a sleek, vintage red muscle car.

I take a few more steps, moving closer to him. "It sounded sexy until you showed me the cover."

He pats the couch at his side and motions for me to sit. "There's only one thing sexier than a hot rod, Jo."

I sit down, leaving a few feet between us for safety. But at this point, I don't know if it's for my safety or his. "What?"

"Women, of course." He smiles, showing off his beautiful white teeth against his olive skin.

"Shocking," I tease, finding myself smiling for the first time since I woke up still filled with alcohol.

He turns, giving me that smile, and my heart stutters in my chest. "I have to go to work in a bit."

"Can I come?" I ask, shocking myself and him, based on the way his eyes widen.

"Wouldn't you rather stay here?"

I shake my head. "I don't want to lie around all day. I'd rather be up and about. Maybe I can help you."

He tilts his head, furrowing those dark-brown brows. "You're going to help me?"

I nod.

"Help me?" He presses his fingers to his chest. "I want to make sure I heard you right."

"Yeah. I can help."

"What the hell do you know about cars?"

"Well..." I pull my legs under my body, relaxing back into the couch. "My dad was a big car guy, and I used to help him when he was around."

"Is he dead?"

"Oh God, no. He isn't around much anymore. He and my mother don't see eye to eye."

"Sorry they're divorced. I can't imagine what that's like," he says, his face softening and his attitude dropping away completely.

"They're still married, but he doesn't come home but maybe once a year for a week, and then he's gone again."

"For real?"

"Yep," I snap, popping the P.

"Why?"

I pull at my sleeve again, covering my fingers. "It's how they want it. It's not something I can explain easily or quickly."

"Sounds fucked up."

I nod, because it is fucked up. "It's not the best situation."

"Where does he live, then?"

"Wherever his work takes him."

"Where is he now?"

I chew on my lip, trying to remember what he said the last time we spoke. He's been shooting in different locations on three continents for his upcoming blockbuster sci-fi movie. "I think he's in Iceland."

He studies me for a moment, blinking and staring. "You think he's in Iceland?"

"I haven't talked to him in two weeks, but that's where he was the last time we spoke."

"Shit," Nick mumbles. "My parents call me every day."

My eyes widen, and my mouth falls open. "Every day?"

He nods but doesn't gloat. "They haven't learned boundaries."

"That must be nice." I wish I had parents who cared about me as much as his care about him. "What do you talk about?"

He moves back, turning his upper body to face me. "They ask me how my day went or tell me the latest family news. We mostly bullshit for a few minutes because I see them every weekend."

"Wait." I hold up my hand. "You see your parents every weekend?"

He slides his arm across the back of the couch, his hand stopping only a few inches from my shoulder. "I see my entire family every weekend."

"Do you guys know it's not the 1950s?" I tease.

"Babe, my grandma is old-school Italian. Sunday dinner is a requirement for every member of the family. No excuses unless you're sick or out of town."

I gape at him, envious of the family life he's been blessed with, while I have none. "Are you lying to me? People really do things like that?"

He smiles, inching his hand closer. "Completely serious."

"So, tomorrow's Sunday, and I guess that means you'll be gone all day?"

He nods. "I've already had the call from my grandmother while you were sleeping, and I have been told I'm required to bring you as my guest if you're still here."

"Me?" I blink. "I don't know..."

"You don't have to, but it'll break my poor old grandmother's heart."

I wrinkle my nose. "You're playing dirty."

He smirks, brushing his fingertips gently over my bare shoulder sticking out from my slouchy, oversized sweatshirt. "It's the only way I play, babe."

My face heats, and there's no doubt my cheeks are bright red by the way his smirk widens into a full-on smile. "Fine. I'll go because I don't believe your family gets together every week."

"You're about to have your mind blown," he tells me, leaving his fingertips on my shoulder. "Now, back to cars and the lie you were telling me about knowing a thing or two about them."

"I'm not lying. I know how to do a few things. The most basic stuff, at least, but I know my tools. I could maybe be your right hand for the day."

His smirk turns even more devilish, and the heat in my face starts to crawl down my neck. "Fine, babe. You can be my right hand all day long."

"At work," I correct him.

"At work, but—" his gaze sweeps over my body "—you should probably put on something you can get dirty in."

I glance down, looking at my sweatshirt and black yoga pants. "This is casual."

He laughs, making my belly flip. "I'll give you an old T-shirt to wear unless you want grease all over that cute pink sweatshirt."

"How exactly do you get grease everywhere? Are you rolling around in it?"

"Go change," he demands, moving his hand away from my shoulder and taking the warmth of his skin with it. "We leave in five."

"Five?" I gasp, scrambling to my feet. "I can't go looking like this." I wave my hand in front of my face and suddenly feel light-headed.

"Whoa," he says, reaching out and grabbing my arm to steady me. "Sit back down." Gently, he guides me back to the couch, keeping his hand on me as I sit. "I think you should stay here and rest."

"I don't want to," I reply, sounding like a bratty little kid. "I'm fine. I'm fine."

He keeps his hand on my arm, holding me in place. "You almost fell over. That is not fine."

"I will be fine," I argue, keeping my voice even, although the touch of his hand on my skin is the only thing I can feel right now.

I'm not worried about the spinning room or the way my stomach is twisting at the very thought of eating something. It's only his hand. Only his warmth.

"Stay here," he tells me, and there's no give in his voice.

"I'll rest and then maybe drop by later and bring you something to eat. Would that be okay?"

His thumb swipes back and forth near my wrist, stealing my breath. "Sounds perfect, babe."

"Off my bed," I tease, trying to put a little distance between us and needing to lie down.

"Nope."

I blink, my smile fading. "No?"

"Nope," he repeats and moves faster than I can react. I'm in his arms, off the couch, being carried toward his bedroom. "I'm not taking a chance of you falling and getting hurt."

"You're kind of overdoing it," I tell him, but I don't mean a word I'm speaking. It's nice to be carried and doted on by a man. It's something I've never experienced. The fact that he is hot doesn't hurt either. "I've survived this long without someone worrying about me."

He gingerly sets me on the mattress, sliding his arms up my back to my head before he stops, and so does my body. "No one's worried about you?"

I bite my lip, trying to stop the frown. "Only Kimberly, but she doesn't count because she works for me."

"Your parents have to worry," he tells me, leaning over me, cradling my head in his big, strong hands.

"They don't. They're too busy worrying about themselves to worry about me, but at least I have Kimberly."

"Sucks, babe," he mutters as he lowers his hand and my head to the pillow.

"It's fine," I say, disregarding the years of neglect from my parents. Neglect no one knows about because my parents are always good at showing their other side to the public and paparazzi.

Nick shoves his hand into his pocket, pulls out his phone, and taps on the screen. His eyes are on me as he says, "Hey, Ma."

He pauses, and my eyes widen.

Why is he calling his mother?

"I'm good." He rakes his eyes over me as I lie on the bed, frozen like I've suddenly become paralyzed. "I was wondering if you could do me a favor?"

"No." I wave my hands in front of him. "Don't do it."

He shakes his head, pushing my hands down in one easy and gentle motion. "I have a friend staying over..." He smiles, winking at me. "Yeah, Ma. A woman friend."

I want to slink away and crawl under the bed, hiding from everything, including his mother.

"She isn't feeling too well. Nothing horrible. A rough night and one too many drinks. I was wondering if you could drop by in a few hours and maybe bring her some soup or something because I have to go to work."

"Nick," I call out, pleading with him to tell her never mind. "Don't ask her to do that. I don't need anyone to bring me food."

He shakes his head again, but this time, he turns his back to me. "Her name's Jo. Let yourself in, and if she's asleep, she'll be in my room." He pauses again, standing completely still. "Yeah, my bed." Again, another long pause as his mother speaks. "No, she's not my girlfriend. We haven't even slept together yet."

Oh. My. God. He said *yet.*

"Nick," I gasp, pulling a pillow over and placing it on my face, unable to even face the world, let alone him or his mother. "I can't believe he said that." My words are muffled in the pillow, but I can hear his laughter.

"Thanks, Ma. You're the best," he tells her before the sound of his feet grows louder as he moves closer to me. "Jo."

I throw my arm over the pillow as soon as it starts to move away from my face. "Go away."

"Don't be that way."

"I can't believe you called your mother," I mumble against the cotton pillowcase. "She's going to think I'm..."

The pillow is gone, and all I see is his face, covered in sunshine, looking like sin. "She's not going to think anything. My mom isn't like that. She's sweet, loving, and a gentle soul. You're making a big deal about nothing."

"Nothing?" I blink, my mouth hanging open.

His fingers come to my chin, pushing my mouth closed. "It's soup."

"You really shouldn't have put her out. I can take care of myself for a few hours. I'm not dying. I'm only hungover. I'm sure she has better things to do."

He smiles, touching my cheek so tenderly, something in my chest flutters. "It'll make her feel useful, and I'll be able to work without worrying about you."

"You don't need to worry about me either."

"Such a hard-ass. Does that steel exterior ever crack?"

"I...I–"

"I didn't think so. I have to go, but Mom will be here in a few hours."

"Okay," I sigh. "I'll be right here."

"Don't do anything stupid."

"Like what?"

He shrugs. "Don't know, but I'm sure you'd figure out something, given half the chance."

Somehow, I stop myself from giving him the middle finger or throwing a smartass comment in his direction. "I'm not moving." I yawn, stretching. "I'll be out before you make it to the driveway."

"Good." He smiles down at me, brushing his fingers one more time against my cheek, and that same weird fluttering hits my chest. "Sweet dreams."

"Have a good day at work."

"Bye, babe."

"Bye."

I stare at his back and then the door after it closes and he disappears. The entire last ten minutes didn't feel like two strangers having a conversation. It felt more like two people who've known each other for a long time. Like two people who were in a relationship. It felt like a man caring for a woman in a deeper way.

Stop being a moron.

We are strangers.

We will always be strangers.

I close my eyes, but there is a smile on my face, because even if we are and always will be strangers, it feels nice to have someone worry about me without expecting anything in return.

9

JO

"SWEETHEART."

I groan, my stomach turning and my head still pounding.

"Jo," a woman says, "wake up."

I flutter my eyes open, immediately blinded by the sunlight. Blinking, I try to focus on the ethereal figure in front of me with her bright-red hair and sunrays behind her, looking like they emanate from her being.

"I brought you some lunch, sweetheart."

I blink again, confused and dazed. "You did?" I ask, my voice still groggy and my throat killing me from earlier.

"I'm Angel," she says softly.

I smile, staring up at her. "You look like one."

She's beautiful and radiant. If Michelangelo ever needed a muse to create his masterpiece in the Sistine Chapel, he'd use her as the perfect specimen.

She smiles back at me, looking every bit as sweet as Nick described her. "Do you need help getting up?"

"No, ma'am," I reply, pushing myself upward with my hands flat on the mattress. "I'm not sick, sick. Just a little..."

"Nick told me. We've all been there, but the nice thing is, it doesn't last too long."

The room doesn't spin when I sit up like it did earlier. I blink away the sleep, trying to find my bearings. "I'm sorry you had to come all this way. I'm really okay."

She waves her hand, keeping that sweet smile on her lips. "It was no trouble. I don't live far away, and I didn't have to work today, so I was busy making dessert for tomorrow anyway."

"You're very kind," I say softly, still feeling guilty.

"Why don't you get yourself together, and I'll prep your soup. Meet me in the kitchen?"

I nod and rub my eyes. "Thank you."

"You don't need to thank me so much. It was really no trouble. Anyway, when Nick said he had a girl friend at his house, I was more than a little curious."

"Friend," I correct her.

"Who's female." She winks and turns, walking out of the room.

I sit there for a minute, staring at the door in a haze before finally making it to my feet. Slowly, I walk to the bathroom, feeling a heaviness in my head and my entire body. When I look in the mirror, I recoil at my reflection.

I look like hell, with bloodshot eyes, makeup half on and half off, smudged across my face.

When I glance down, there's a washcloth on top of a stack of towels, along with a new toothbrush. Nick. The guy thinks of everything. Maybe he keeps a drawer of toothbrushes for the countless women who, no doubt, make their way in and out of his bed on a regular basis. I am probably the first one he didn't have sex with who received the morning care package.

A few minutes later, with a freshly washed face and a new change of clothes, I make my way to the kitchen. Nick's mom is standing at the stove, stirring the soup she's made in a small pot.

"Feel better?" she asks as I slide onto a stool around his kitchen island.

"Much better," I tell her, moving my hand to my stomach as it grumbles from the delicious smell.

"Good." She turns and smiles at me. "I made chicken noodle. Easy on the stomach."

"Homemade?" I ask, because who whips up a pot of homemade chicken noodle soup at the last minute? No one I know, especially none of my friends' parents, who are also too busy with their careers to go to those great lengths.

Her back is to me when she says, "Of course."

She says of course like it's crazy to think any other way. I grew up making myself a small pot of chicken soup that was dehydrated and came from a tiny packet and a red box.

"Of course," I whisper back.

I sit in silence, watching her as she grabs a bowl, dishing out a hefty helping of the chicken soup she created with her own two hands. She slides it across the counter, immediately crouching down to rest her head on her palm. "I hope you like it."

I reach for the spoon that had been laid out for me before I sat down. "Aren't you having any?"

She shakes her head. "I ate already, and I'm not much of a soup lover."

So, not only was she selfless in making me homemade soup, but she cooked something she had no interest in ever eating herself. Man, Nick doesn't know how great he has it, having a mother who cares this much about him. I'm pretty damn sure every time he didn't feel good, he was made the same chicken soup by the same loving mother.

"It smells amazing." I peer down at the huge chunks of carrots, celery, potatoes, chicken, and more than enough noodles to satisfy any eater.

"Eat. Eat," she tells me.

I grab the spoon, immediately digging in.

"Blow on it first," she offers, and my heart is heavy because she's so sweet, exactly like you'd expect a mother to be. "I don't want you to burn your mouth."

"Thank you," I repeat, cringing as soon as the words are out of my mouth.

"It's fine. Old habits die hard, baby."

Blowing on the soup, I sneak a peek in her direction,

seeing her watching me, studying my face. I bend my neck, facing my soup, avoiding her gaze as I place the spoon in my mouth, and all the flavors explode across my tongue.

"So, how did you meet Nick?" she asks before I have a chance to swallow.

I hold up a finger, savoring every morsel that's in my mouth a little longer than is probably necessary because I don't want to answer. "Oh my God, this is so good."

"It's nothing. Only simple chicken noodle."

"No. No. It's absolute perfection," I reply, trying to stay off the topic of Nick and me.

"So, Nick..."

Damn. "I was on vacation, and there was a problem at my hotel. He overheard and offered me a place to stay for the night."

She stares at me for a minute, tilting her head. "And you were drunk when this happened?"

"No. I was drunk last night because of his cousins and my inability to say no."

Angel's face lights up. "Put those four together, and it always spells trouble."

"I figured that out the hard way."

"So, that means you've been here more than a night?"

"Two."

Two days and I've already met his cousins and his mother. She's made me soup. He's seen me puke. And none of them seem fazed by any of this, nor are they judging me for my choices or poor life decisions.

She studies me again, tapping one set of fingers against the stone countertop.

"Did I do something wrong?" I ask.

She smiles, shaking her head. "You didn't do anything wrong. I'm surprised by you being here is all."

"Well, yeah. I'm sure your son having a stranger stay in his house is disconcerting."

She laughs softly. "It's not that. Nick can and does take care of himself. It's only that Nick..."

"Shit. Is he gay?" I ask, my eyes widening because I hadn't thought of that. He's so flirty, but maybe he's sweet like his mom. He hasn't made any moves on me. Innuendo, yes, but nothing actually physical.

Her laugh grows louder, and then she sobers. "Baby, I wouldn't care if my son were gay as long as he was happy. But no, Nick is not gay. He's always been a ladies' man."

"So, then..."

"Nick has never had a woman sleep over. He has a lot of rules about sex and relationships, and one of them is no sleepovers."

I furrow my brows, confused. "What? Why?"

"He says it complicates feelings." She shrugs. "Men. They're a conundrum."

"Well, technically, we aren't in a relationship, nor are we having sex. I'm a stranger or maybe a new friend, but a couple...we are not."

"There's a reason he doesn't even have beds in his two spare bedrooms. He doesn't like houseguests of any kind. So, you see, you being here is...different for him."

I stare at her, blinking and confused. "I'm only passing through."

"Uh-huh," she mutters, smiling at me like she knows something I don't. "Having my homemade chicken soup and sleeping in his bed."

"Well... I... Uh..." I pause, allowing myself to get my bearings. We aren't anything more. We haven't even kissed or embraced. He is being nice, and I am passing through. "I slept on the couch the night before."

She winks at me with those eyes. "Keep telling yourself whatever you want to make yourself feel better. I know my Nicky better than anyone, probably even better than he knows himself."

I swallow, frozen for a second. "You think..."

She shakes her head. "I think nothing." Her smile says otherwise.

"Eat. You need some meat on your bones."

I frown. "I've been on a diet for a few weeks."

The look of horror on her face is unmistakable. "Why?"

I lift the spoon toward my lips. "I work in Hollywood, and my publicist said I needed to lose a few pounds. Cameras aren't friendly."

Her hand slides across the countertop, coming to a rest on top of my arm. Her eyes meet mine, boring into me, but her face is soft and sweet. "Beauty comes from inside, honey, not the outside."

"If only it were that simple. But thank you, Angel."

"Come to dinner tomorrow," she offers, giving my

arm a squeeze. "You can take a day off your diet and have some of the best homemade Italian cooking you'll ever taste."

"I don't know. That may be crossing a line Nick doesn't want to cross."

"You're his friend, right?"

I nod.

"He's brought friends before."

"Girls?"

"Well—" she mutters, smirking. "—no. But you're still only friends, and we'll make sure everyone knows that too."

"I don't know, Angel."

"It's decided. Family dinner tomorrow at Grandma's house."

I stare at her, knowing I won't be able to win this argument. "Okay," I promise, giving in. "I'll come."

Her smile widens. "Perfect."

10

NICK

MAMMOTH LIFTS HIS HEAD, STARING AT ME. "How long's she staying?"

I shrug, wiping the grease off my hands. "Don't know, man. Don't care. She's kind of nice to have around."

He raises an eyebrow, smirking. "She got you."

"What?"

"She got you, man."

"She doesn't have me, asswipe."

"After half a decade of kickin' pussy out of your bed, you're letting pussy that you haven't even tasted stay in your bed. She got you."

I glare at him, wiping my hands a little harder than before. "Again, jagoff, she doesn't *have* me. She's only staying a couple days, and she was sick last night. Was I supposed to leave her on the couch?"

He points at me with a smug grin. "Tell yourself whatever lies you need, but she got you. I don't care who the chick is. If I don't love her, her ass *is* on the couch and not in my bed, sick or not."

My lips harden along with my glare. "You talk a big game, but you're one big pussy too. I know how you are with my cousin. You're as whipped as the next guy."

"I know I'm whipped, but I've had a lot of years and miles to get to his point. You're whipped, and it's been what..." He pauses, laughing louder. "Two fuckin' days."

"You're an asshole," I snap, walking away from him.

The speaker in the garage comes on, making the hideous noise it always does. "Nicky, you have a visitor," Tamara calls out with glee in her voice. "She's waiting for you in the parking lot."

"Pussy-whipped in under forty-eight," Mammoth mutters as soon as the microphone kicks out.

"Fuck off," I bite out, throwing the rag on my tool chest. "You were pussy-whipped from the moment you met my cousin, but you keep pretending you weren't chasing her tail."

"Oh. I know what I am and when I was, but as soon as you come to terms with the fact that there's something brewing deep inside you for this chick you barely know, the better off you'll be."

I throw up a middle finger as I head out of the garage, leaving Mammoth and his words of wisdom behind. Jo's sitting on the hood of her car with a brown paper bag at her side. She looks more casual than I've ever seen her. with her palms resting next to her legs, body bent forward slightly.

She looks like a vision in the dimming sunlight of the late evening. The sky blazes with shades of blue, pink, orange, and yellow, giving her the ultimate backdrop to show off the beauty she no doubt knows she has.

As if sensing my presence, she lifts her head, her eyes locking with mine. For a moment, neither of us says anything as I move toward her, my footsteps fast and loud on the sticky blacktop.

"Hey." There's a faint smile playing on her lips as she drinks me in with those blue eyes. "I promised you dinner, and I didn't forget."

My eyes move to the bag and then back to her. "You should be resting."

"I was hungover, Nick, not sick. I'm fine now."

I stop moving a few feet away, letting my gaze dip to her tanned legs, which are shown off in the most spectacular way in her black shorts. "Mom come by?" I ask.

Her face brightens at the mention of my mom. "Yep. She makes the best chicken noodle soup I've ever had the pleasure of eating."

"My mom is an okay cook. The best soup ever?" I laugh, swiping my hands down the front of my shirt. "You clearly haven't had that many home-cooked meals."

The frown on her face is immediate. "No. No, I haven't," she utters, dropping her face back toward her legs, watching her feet swing back and forth.

"Hey," I say, closing the space between us until my stomach touches her knees and my fingers find her chin. "I didn't mean to be an asshole."

"It's fine," she says, fighting my touch and not giving me her blue eyes.

"Jo," I reply. "It wasn't fair of me to say."

"It was the truth, though." She lifts her head, my fingers still at her chin, staring at me with those dark eyes. "My life isn't glamorous. People see what they want. They only see the privilege and the money. Never the loneliness or the lack of family. My parents are great at trotting me out for a photo op but pretty much shit at everything else."

"I'm sorry," I repeat, my stomach knotting at her words and the sadness hidden so deep, if you weren't looking, you'd totally miss it.

"You grew up with parents who cared. A mother who loved you enough to make you soup. Cousins who liked you and wanted to hang out, even after they've seen you at work or the day before. You, no doubt, have aunts and uncles who fawned over you. Do you know what I had?" She lifts her chin higher, almost defensively, as her fingers curl around the hood of her car.

"I'm guessing not much."

"I had a nanny, a maid, and a chauffeur. I didn't have parents who cared beyond me keeping my image clean so we didn't make the papers, and the rest of the family stopped talking to my parents when I was young. So, I had three people, all of whom were paid to pay attention to me."

I suck in a breath, feeling her words like a punch to the gut. "I can't imagine."

"No. You can't, and for that, I'm thankful. It may not be the worst thing in the world, I know I had it better than most, but it doesn't give a person the warm fuzzies."

Without even thinking, I move forward, pushing her legs apart with my hand and nestling my hips against her knees. My arms are around her, holding her. As if we've done this a hundred times, she folds her face into my neck, her lips pressing against my skin. I flatten my palms against her back, rubbing her gently. "Babe, you got the shit end of the stick."

There is silence for a good ten seconds, and then her body starts to shake, followed by the hum of her laughter flowing out of her lips and against my neck. "Shit end of the stick? What does that even mean?" she asks, pulling back but not away, only far enough so she can see my eyes.

"Fuck if I know." I smile, soaking in her beauty while her guard is down as I slide my hands closer to her neck. "Just something we say."

Her hands finally move from the car to my sides, gripping on to me tightly. "Maybe someday I'll be as blessed as you and have a family of my own. Then I can do things right and vanquish all the bad shit from my childhood. One can cancel out the other, yeah?"

I give her neck a light squeeze, resisting the urge to kiss her. "You deserve that and more, babe."

Her shoulders relax, and her head falls forward to my shoulder. "You know," she adds, her face tipped toward where our bodies meet. "Underneath your crabby exterior and tough-guy bravado, you're really sweet."

I squeeze her neck again, smiling. "I am what I am, and I don't have bravado."

She lifts her head again, her eyes searching my face, her lips twitching.

I stare back at her, my face unmoving and emotionless.

"See," she teases, her face breaking into a full-on smile. "That right there is what I'm talking about."

"Babe, it's my face. I can't change it."

She laughs softly. "It's your stony façade," she teases, pausing for a second as her face softens and her laugh quiets. "But when you smile, you could light up a room with the warmth that emanates from you."

"You use a lot of flowery words. But coming out of your mouth, they sound like the most beautiful compliment even if they're said after something so—"

"I've never said anything mean," she cuts me off, sliding her hands up my sides until they're on my ribs. She sucks in a breath, our eyes locked, and the air grows thick. "You're unlike anyone I've ever met before, Nicky."

There's a heaviness in my chest from the way my name rolls off her tongue, and her gaze dips to my mouth before slowly gliding upward and back to my eyes. "I can say the same about you, Jo."

"I'm boring," she sighs, slouching forward again.

Moving one of my hands, I find her chin, always forcing her to look at me when anything gets too real or when she talks down about herself. I never would've guessed the woman doesn't think highly of herself. Someone who comes from money or Hollywood, I always assumed was full of themselves. Maybe she was or at least had been, but being around me and the realness of my family has placed some cracks in her carefully polished and practiced veneer.

When her eyes meet mine again, I shake my head. "Don't do that."

"What?" she asks.

"You're not boring, babe. There's something deep inside you, something you've hidden for far too long, that's dying to come out. There's a wildcat in there, prowling the perimeter, ready to break free and explore the world outside their perfectly crafted cosmos."

She blinks as her lips pull down. "I don't have the luxury of breaking free."

"Babe." I move closer as she slides her hands around my back, locking her fingers together. "Here, you can be whatever you want to be. Here, you can do whatever you want to do. You're not in Hollywood anymore. You're not under the thumb of your parents, their people, or the prying eyes of the media. We're surrounded by trees, rednecks, and nothing but road. You want to explore that wildcat, I'm the man to help you bring out that side of you."

She stares at me, her eyes locked on my mouth as I speak. "I don't..."

Fuck, the heat from her body overpowers the warmth

of the sun and the humid Florida air around us. Everything else fades away, including the sounds of power tools coming from the garage. All that matters in this moment is us. All that matters is that she feels like she can be whoever or whatever she wants when she's with me. I won't judge her on her life choices—except for Jamison; he'll always be a fucking tool.

She's so beautiful in this light, and the way she's staring at my mouth tells me one thing; she wants to add me to the list of living life on the edge and exploring a side of herself she never has before. "I'm going to kiss you now."

"I..." Her eyes flicker to mine, widening. "I..."

"Yes or no? Simple answer."

She swallows, eyes still wide, and nods. "Yes," she breathes, holding my gaze as she licks her lips. "Please."

I tighten my hand around the back of her neck, the other still on her face, sliding up her cheek. When I bend forward, she tilts her head to the side, closing her eyes, waiting for the moment our mouths meet.

I'd be lying if I didn't admit to myself that my stomach is knotting in the same way it used to when I was nervous before a big game. My chest tightens, my cock grows hard, and I pull her face to mine before crushing my lips against hers.

Her arms tighten around my middle as I curl my fingers around her neck with my palm against her cheek.

I breathe in the sweet smell of her skin as I take her

mouth hard and fast, leaving no room for doubt that I want her.

The moan that escapes her lips sends signals firing throughout my body, ending straight at my dick. I kiss her deeper, wanting more of that sound, more of the feeling the simple noise caused in my body.

As she curls her fingers around my T-shirt, lifting it from my skin, the air no longer feels cool. Her skin finds mine, scorching me with the lightest touch.

I tangle my hand in her hair, tipping her head back, letting my tongue slip deeper as hers dances around mine in the most carnal of movements.

A click off to the side whirs in my ears like the annoying buzz of a mosquito, but I can't stop. I won't stop. I've wanted to kiss her since the moment she was curled up on my couch, hair a mess, face smashed into the pillow, looking so damn cute it made my balls ache.

Another click and Jo freezes, pulling back, eyes opening and then widening. "Oh my God," she mumbles with her lips swollen from my kiss. She glances around, her head moving fast, scanning our surroundings. "Fuck. They found me." Her hands pull away a second later, pushing against my chest a moment after that. "I have to go."

"Wait," I blurt out, reaching for her, grabbing her by the arm as she tries to shimmy off the hood of the car, scrambling to her feet.

She yanks her arm free of my grip. "I can't do this. I

have to go. I have to go. I have to go," she repeats, moving frantically toward her driver's side door.

"Jo, wait," I plead, holding out my hand. "I'll take care of whatever it is."

Another click.

My eyes follow hers to a black lens peeking out from the side of a tree at the garage's property line.

"What the fuck?"

"Photographers are the scum of the earth," she mumbles, sliding into her car seat. "I'm sorry, Nick."

"Sorry?" I scratch my head, dick still hard, lips wet from her mouth being on mine. "Don't go."

She sticks out her arm, curling her fingers around the inside handle of her car door. "Thanks for being you and showing me there's more out there than I knew possible," she says, slamming the door and closing herself off from me and the prying eyes of the asshat hiding behind the tree.

I barely take a breath before she fires up her car, peeling back, my dinner falling to the blacktop near my feet, and she takes off, driving away like she is in a race for her life.

I growl, curling my fingers into my palms, stalking toward the dickhead who interrupted a beautiful moment and my dinner date for the evening.

"Hey!"

A man with black hair and his baseball hat turned backward backs away, taking quick steps.

I advance, moving faster, not willing to let him get away. "Stop!"

He runs, but I run faster, my legs a good six inches longer than his, needing fewer steps to cover the same ground.

"Don't!" he screams, lifting up his camera and his hands. "Don't hit me. I'll sue."

I slow my steps to a trot until I am within arm's reach, ready to swing on him, lawsuit or not. "What the fuck, dude? What gives you the right to come on to my property and invade our privacy? Tell me one good reason why I shouldn't beat your ass right here, and don't mention a lawsuit because I can guarantee I have the law on my side around these parts."

He swallows, still holding his hands up in the air, the camera in one hand. "Technically, I was never on your property."

"You're not giving me a good reason not to knock your lights out."

"I'm only doing my job, man. I take photos. That's it. I only know who, but not what or how. I'm trying to make a living and feed my kids."

Fuck. I knew Jo had something cooking in California. I knew her parents were important and had some form of celebrity status, but when she had mentioned photographers followed her around, I thought she was pulling my leg. Never in a million years did I think they'd be hiding behind trees, trying to take a photo of her doing something tabloid-worthy.

I reach back, going for my wallet. "How much to make sure those photos never see the light of day?"

The man's eyes follow my hands, and I can see the hunger in them. He's driven by greed and nothing else. A man like him is easily bought. "Two thousand."

I tilt my head, blinking at him. "Two grand for some photos of us kissing?"

"I could get more from my publisher, but for you, I'm willing to give you a discount. I'd really hate for some of these to make the front page."

"Front page," I grumble, glancing toward the sky. "Who cares what Jo does? It's completely ridiculous."

"You know who she is, right?"

"Of course," I scoff, pulling out five one-hundred-dollar bills from my wallet, knowing I'll have to go to the office and beg Tamara to lend me the other fifteen hundred.

"Who is she, then?" he asks, sounding snide and not at all worried anymore that I'm going to punch him square in the jaw.

"She's Jo. Her parents are celebrities."

He laughs, shaking his head. "She's Josephine Carmichael."

"And?"

"Carmichael," he repeats, but slower like I'm a freaking moron. "Her parents are not only celebrities. They are *the* celebrity couple of the decade. Not only that, but her grandparents were Hollywood legends, too.

That doesn't make her a celebrity, but Hollywood royalty."

"Carmichael," I mumble to myself. "Carmichael."

The name is familiar, but Hollywood isn't my thing. Celebrities aren't my thing either. Never have been, and never would be. I don't give two fucks what happens on the other side of the country where tofu-eating barefoot hippies dance on the beach, smoking weed, and communing with God.

"Madeline and Michael Carmichael," he tells me, being more specific. "Four Oscars, twelve Golden Globes, and more films than I can count. Those Carmichaels."

"Carmichael," I repeat, shaking my head. "I mean, I kind of know who they are, but it's not my thing, man. All I care about is those photos don't leave this property."

He holds out his hand, and I place the bills against his palm. "You're light."

"I'll get the rest, but you'll have to give me a minute to grab it."

He glances toward the garage. "I'll stay here while you get it."

"Whatever," I mumble, stalking away, more pissed than I was before.

Not at Jo, she is the innocent in this, but at the douchebag that holds her life in his hands and profits off her happiness or misfortune. What a shit way to live. I can't imagine being followed, always looking over my shoulder to make sure I'm not being followed or there isn't someone holding out their cell phone, looking for the most inopportune moment to change my life with the simple click of a button.

I peer over my shoulder at the cocksucker, standing near the street, a smug grin on his face. He shoves the money into his pocket and waves, rubbing my face in the fact that he has me by the shorthairs.

Part of me doesn't care who sees the photos.

But the other part of me, the part that had his lips planted on her, drowning in her warmth, wants to give the guy the money and then beat him into the ground so he'll think twice before following her again.

It was a kiss.

Only a kiss.

There is nothing salacious in something so simple and beautiful.

But I know, somehow, the prick is going to make it look more sinful than it really was, doing everything possible to ruin Jo in the process.

11

NICK

"What the hell do you need fifteen hundred dollars for?" Tamara blinks, her mouth hanging open. "That's a lot of money, Nicky."

I lean over the counter in the office, trying to keep my temper in check. "Don't ask, Tam. Give it to me, and I'll have it back in the till by the end of the day."

"Did a bet go bad?"

I tilt my head, staring at her. "What? No. I need it for something I hadn't expected."

"Twenty bucks is for something you didn't expect. Fifteen hundred is for something you brought upon yourself, and not in the good way either."

I clench my jaw, talking through my teeth. "Tam, I don't have time for this shit. I'll go to the bank and get you the money right after."

She purses her lips and glares at me. "Why can't you go to the bank now? What's the rush?" Her eyes flicker to the security cameras, spotting the man standing next to the tree. "Is it him?" She points at the screen and leans forward to get a better look.

"Maybe," I grumble, peering up at the ceiling, cursing under my breath.

"Well," she says, "you don't have to worry about the money because he took off."

I almost fly over the desk, trying to get a look at the screen. "What? Where?"

"There." She points him out, nothing but his back visible to the camera as he heads into the parking lot of the small corner store next to our property. "And, he's gone," she groans as he slides into a car.

"Fuck!" I hiss, slamming my hands down on the countertop. "Asshole has my five hundred bucks and the photos."

Tamara's eyes flicker to mine as her eyebrows draw downward. "Photos?"

"Of me and Jo." I shake my head, running my fingers through my hair. "Goddamn it."

She blinks, staring at me in total confusion. "What in the hell does he want photos of you two kissing for?"

I pinch the bridge of my nose, wishing I hadn't let that lying prick out of my sight. "Fucking shit."

"Seriously, why?"

"Do you know who the Carmichaels are?"

"The old couple down the street from Grandma and Grandpa?"

I shake my head. "No. The Carmichaels in Hollywood."

She stares at me for a second with a blank expression, her eyes blinking open and closed, open and closed. "Um," she mumbles, but then her eyes widen. "You mean Madeline and Michael Carmichael, like, the biggest celebrity couple of all time?"

"Those would be the ones."

She glances around, looking like someone smacked into her and she was stunned. "And what about them? I'm so confused."

"They're Jo's parents."

She gasps, covering her mouth with her hand. "Oh. My. God. Jo is Josephine Carmichael, heir to the Carmichael dynasty and fortune."

I sigh, rolling my eyes, biting back the anger that's at a full-on boil inside of me. "A bit dramatic, aren't you?"

She shakes her head as she stands, bringing her face close to me. "Nicky, she's not the kid of a celebrity, she's a celebrity unto herself. I don't know how I didn't recognize her when we were at the bar, but *fuck me*, it is her."

"Cousin, she's a person like me and you."

Tamara raises one of her perfect, dark eyebrows. "She is not a person. She's way more than that. I've been following her for years."

"And somehow you didn't recognize her?"

"Well, she looks different in person and without all the makeup and filters."

"What the fuck is a filter?" I ask.

She lifts her phone and shakes it in my face. "You know, on a camera to make you look better."

I blink, feeling stupid. "People use filters to look better?"

"Men are clueless creatures." She shakes her head, rolling her eyes. "Where's Jo?"

"She peeled out of here as soon as she spotted the photographer."

"The correct term is paparazzi," she says.

"Whatever," I mutter.

"You're about to become famous too."

"Fucking fantastic," I grumble, pacing the tile floor in front of the counter. "I have to go. Jo had to go back to my place."

"She's going to run."

I stop moving, turning my eyes toward my cousin. "To where?"

She shrugs. "Anywhere she can't be found."

"Fuck!" I howl, hauling ass out of the office, knowing Tamara's fucking right.

Seventeen long minutes later, I pull into an empty driveway and run inside the house, frantically searching for her. Her pink suitcase is gone, and any remnant of her being at my place has vanished except for a small white sheet of paper folded on the pillow on the couch with the word *Nick* scrolled in immaculate penmanship.

I grab the note, flip it open, and scan the words.

Nick,

Thank you for the escape, the safety, and the reality.

I'll cherish the short time we had together. I'm sorry for any trouble I've caused you.

You deserve better than to be dragged into the mess I call my life. Your generosity and warmth will never be forgotten.

Always,

Jo xoxo

The paper dangles between my fingers as I move around the house, anger welling up inside me, threatening to boil over.

Fuck.

She is gone. Vanished. Disappeared like she was never here, with only a note as a reminder and the faint smell of her still on my skin.

No matter how hard I try to shake the imprint she made on me, I find it impossible for my mind not to drift back to the moment our lips touched and so many things were spoken without words.

Jesus. I sound like a wishy-washy chick who's fallen head over heels for someone without even really knowing them at all.

I pull out my phone, calling the one person I know can help me find someone on the run. "Dad," I say as soon as he answers. "I need your help."

"What's up, Nick?" he replies without hesitation.

"You know the woman who was at my house earlier today?"

"The one your mother brought over soup to?"

"Yeah."

"Mmm-hmm. Your mother grew rather fond of her in the short time they spent together."

"She's gone, and I need to find her."

"I see someone else is as fond of her as your mother."

"Dad."

"Son."

"Dad, will you help me?"

"Why did she leave?"

"She's not who I thought."

"Say that again," he tells me, and I cringe because that sounded way shittier than it really is.

"Her parents are famous."

I pause, and my father clicks his tongue.

"And, I guess, she's famous too," I tell him. "Someone snapped a photo of us today, and she took off."

"She's probably blowing off some steam, Nick. She'll probably be back. Having your privacy invaded like that on a constant basis isn't easy for anyone. You may need to give her space if you're looking for her to return."

"Dad, she took all her shit and left a note. She's not coming back."

"Maybe it's best to let sleeping dogs lie."

"I'm going to pretend you didn't say that. I won't accept that she's gone and there's nothing I can do about it. I need to know she's okay. I need to know she's safe. I need to..."

"Sounds like more than fondness, son. She got under your skin faster than I ever thought possible."

Damn. She did.

She slid in there when I was looking at her sweet smiles, and then the kiss...the kiss was the end of me.

I blow out a breath, feeling winded and like someone punched me right in the gut. "She's in deep, and I don't think I'll ever get her hook out of me without at least knowing she's okay."

"You sure she wants you coming after her?"

I glance up, closing my eyes, holding the phone to my ear. "Whatever she wants. I can't force her to be here if she wants to run, but I need to know she isn't driving around frantically, sleeping in another parking lot tonight. Shit ain't safe for a woman."

"You're letting your sexism show, Nicholas."

"She doesn't have a gun. I'm pretty sure any senior citizen within a fifty-mile radius could beat her in a physical fight. So, yeah, I may sound sexist, but I'm only speaking the truth. She can't be out there alone, sleeping in a dark parking lot."

"There are hotels."

"Motels," I correct him. "She's a Ritz kind of girl."

"So, then head south. I'm sure you'll find her near Clearwater."

"Old man, you're going to make me drive around two counties trying to track down a woman you can find with a simple phone call."

He scoffs. "A simple phone call and a favor owed for asking for that information."

"I'll pay your marker. The favor will be owed by me."

"Doesn't work that way."

"You going to do it or not?"

"Consider it done, because if I told you no, your mother would make me pay for the rest of my life."

"Whatever it takes. She was my next call if you said no."

"You don't play fair. But then, you never did."

"Get the info and call me back," I tell him, ending the call and heading out of the house toward my truck.

Fuck the bike.

It isn't practical with the dark clouds forming, the usual evening thunderstorms rolling in when the warm air meets the cooler wind from the Gulf.

Climbing into my truck, I turn the key, gun the engine, and head out toward the taco stand where I first saw her.

"FOUND HER," my father blurts as soon as I pick up. "Sorry it took so long."

"It's been an hour," I bite out, pissed as fuck after driving around for the entire sixty minutes and coming up empty. "I've looked everywhere and can't find her."

"Relax, kid. She didn't get too far in an hour."

"Where is she?" I growl, unable to stop myself because he's dragging his feet.

"She's at the Neon Cowboy."

"The Neon Cowboy? For fuck's sake." I run my hand

down the front of my face, shaking my head. "What the fuck is she doing at a biker bar?"

"Probably drinking and doing her best to get lost in a crowd."

"Dad, she wouldn't blend in with the guys there and not even the women. She'll stick out like a sore thumb."

"Then you better haul ass and go rescue the girl."

"On it. Call me if she moves."

"Been there going on thirty-plus minutes. I don't see her moving any time soon. Good luck."

"Thanks," I say, ending the call and tossing my phone on the passenger seat.

With her looks and designer clothes, the men at the Neon Cowboy would be all over her, and every woman in the place would be plotting her death. Most likely, they'd have no clue who she was, but that wouldn't matter. She'd still be the object of their attention, and the very thought of someone laying hands on her, trying to take advantage of her, makes my stomach turn.

If something happens to her, heads will roll.

12

JO

There's no mistaking the simple fact that I'm not in California or, for that matter, not even in Clearwater, Florida, either.

If I thought I was in the middle-of-nowhere Florida before, I was wrong. This dive bar filled with guys covered in leather and denim, sporting long beards, and covered in tattoos is beyond anything I could've imagined when I stepped foot inside.

Ignoring all the eyes on me, I hop up on a high-top stool in front of the bar, tossing my Louis bag next to me and resting my hand on top.

My gaze follows the bartender, a man who's easily one of the largest guys I've ever laid eyes on, as he pours drinks and sweet-talks some of the female patrons down the row from me. He's sporting a *Ride or Die* tank top that used to be a T-shirt before someone took a pair of scissors to the material, cutting off the sleeves.

I don't need to look around to know most of the eyes in the place are still pointed in my direction. I've been the center of attention on more than one occasion, but usually surrounded by the media and Hollywood elite.

This experience is different.

I feel like an outsider in every way. Usually bartenders are an easy mark, always willing to bend over backward to serve me first. But not here. Nope. His taste is clearly more trashy than classy.

"Hey, I'd..." I say as he passes by me, holding up a hand to get his attention.

But it doesn't work. I don't even get a sideways glance as he stalks by, heading toward the cooler at the other end of the bar.

"Sir," I call out, waving my hand this time, figuring maybe he can't hear me over the classic rock playing overhead.

Again, I'm wrong as he walks back the other direction to a pair of girls whose hair is teased so high and looks so hard, they have to use an entire bottle of hair spray every time they do their hair.

"Whatcha want, sweetheart?" a man offers, sliding onto the empty stool next to me.

I stop moving, scared to glance his way until he snakes his arm around my high-top stool and his hand touches my back.

"Sir," I reply, putting on my sweet voice as I turn to him. I suck in a breath as my belly plummets, but not in that oh-God-he's-so-sexy kind of way. "I appreciate the offer."

"Didn't offer anything." He gives me a toothy grin as he rakes his eyes over me in the greediest and thirstiest fashion. "Not yet, at least. I asked what you want, not what I want."

"Um," I mumble, soaking in his wild beard that hasn't been trimmed in months. His lips are almost invisible through the strands of hair that seem to point in every direction like a scattered spider web. "Just a whiskey."

"On the rocks?" He raises a bushy eyebrow.

I nod, swallowing down my fear. "It doesn't matter as long as it's liquor."

I see his teeth again because he's smiling. Or at least, I think he is, but it's hard to tell other than the way his cheeks rise and the whiteness of his teeth in between the beard.

"Clay, the woman wants a whiskey on the rocks," he calls out after snapping his fingers at the bartender, getting his attention.

Clay, the asshat who has been ignoring me, gives the burly guy next to me a quick nod and goes about his business.

"I'm going to give you a little advice," the man next to me says, moving his arm away from my back and placing both hands on the bar top in front of him. "Take it for what it's worth, or ignore what I'm about to tell you entirely."

"Everyone has advice and wants to tell me how to run

my life," I mumble, closing my eyes and shaking my head. "Twenty-some years I've been bossed around, and now some stranger wants to sit next to me and give me advice too."

Clay, the dickhead with the cutoff sleeves, slides the drink in front of me, giving the bearded guy to my right the side-eye.

"I see someone ruffled your feathers," the man states, ignoring Clay, as he pushes my drink closer. "Drink up. I think you may need more than one to deal with whatever demon you have inside of you."

"Demon?" I ask, turning my gaze toward him, staring into his eyes that are almost as dark as the blackest sky. My laugh starts small, bubbling out of me louder the more serious his face becomes.

"Lots of demons," he mutters, studying my face as he runs his nubby fingers over his beard. "Might take at least three drinks to have those spirits start talking before giving your mind a rest."

My laughter dies, and I stare at him in confusion. "I appreciate the drink, mister."

"Tobias."

"What?"

"Name's Tobias, not mister."

"I appreciate the drink, Tobias," I correct my previous statement and continue on with where I was going before he felt the need to interject his name. "But I really came here to be alone and think."

"Best thinking is done with a partner."

I blink, wondering if he's crazy, drunk, or a combo of the two. He's making abso-freaking-lutely no sense at all, talking in circles about nonsense. I shake my head and turn my body toward my drink, wrapping my fingers around the cool glass. "While I agree sometimes having someone to bounce your problems off is nice, I need to be with myself tonight."

"Steel," he grunts.

"What?" I blink, remembering when Nick muttered the same thing about me. "I'm not steel," I tell him, lifting my glass to my lips.

"Hard as a rock," he adds, turning his entire body my direction until his knees touch my thighs. "Soft-looking, but beyond that, nothing but stone."

I blink, turning my head only slightly, and stare at him out of the corner of my eyes with the glass still at my lips.

"Listen," he continues, lifting his arm and placing his hand on the back of my stool again, but this time not touching me. "Nothing about you screams biker bar or even that you're looking to take a ride on the wild side tonight, sweetheart."

"Whatever gave you that impression?" I mutter into my glass, staring at the ice cubes as the liquid slowly disappears.

He chuckles, sounding sweet compared to his rough exterior. "No one looking like you strolls into a place like this. So, that means one of two things. Either some dipshit broke your heart, or you're lost. I'm pretty sure the Yelp review doesn't talk about the great food, the fancy drinks, and the impeccable service."

I don't know why, but I laugh and turn my head, placing my drink back on the bar. "Yelp? You use Yelp?"

"Doesn't everyone?" he says, like I'm the crazy one out of the two of us.

"Tobias, what's your endgame here?" I say with a sigh.

"No endgame. You're lost, and this isn't the place someone ever comes to when they want to be found. And since you look like you, I figured you needed someone to sit here by your side, so some horny dipshit doesn't saddle up to you, trying to get into those cute little shorts you're wearing."

He is partially right. I don't want to be found. I wasn't lost, heading down the country road, making a run for the highway to get the hell out of here. But when I saw the row of bikes and the bar after miles of nothing, I stopped to take a break and gather my thoughts.

I ignore him, going back to nursing my whiskey, hoping he'll go away.

"So, where ya from? Sounds West Coast."

"California."

"What part?"

"Near LA."

"I spent a few years in San Diego. Miss the weather out there."

"You lived in California?" I eye him again, wondering

how he fit in with the bohemian lifestyle and cool coastal vibe down in SoCal.

"I was stationed there for three years."

"Navy?" I raise an eyebrow, looking at him a bit differently.

"Yes, ma'am. Spent twenty years serving this country. Lived everywhere. Been to every continent on this planet, wearing the flag, representing our great nation."

"Thanks for your service."

He waves his hand. "I'd like to say I did it for honorable reasons, but it was a paycheck, health insurance, and the only thing I ever knew from the time I was eighteen until almost forty."

"And now?"

"Now, I have my freedom and the wind."

"Freedom," I echo. "I wish I knew what that felt like."

He raises his eyebrows. "Babe, you're not free?"

I shrug. "In the simplest form, I am, but the reality of my freedom and yours are two very different things."

"Husband?"

I shake my head. "Family."

"The worse type of captivity." Tobias motions toward Clay and then to my glass. "Is your family the reason you're sitting your pretty little ass next to me tonight?"

I'm partially flattered, but mostly not. Looking around the bar, the ladies are far from glamorous. Many of them haven't stepped out of the eighties, though their wrinkles have moved forward even if their hair and makeup have not. "Kinda, but it's mostly about a guy."

Tobias's dark eyes study my face for a moment as he leans back. "He break your heart?"

"No. I ran away."

He tilts his head, his eyes narrowing. "He hurt you?"

"No," I snap. "He'd never do that."

"Cheat?"

"No."

"Steal?"

"No."

"You cheat?"

"No."

"You hit him?"

"No."

"Then what the fuck, sweetheart? I'm not trying to be mean, but not for nothing, I don't see why you ran, leaving the poor sap in the dust."

I straighten my back and curl my fingers around the new glass that's placed in front of me by Clay. "My life is complicated, and he didn't need the hassle."

Tobias shakes his head, cursing under his breath. "Did you let him make that decision, or did you go off half-cocked, taking it upon yourself to decide what he wanted or didn't in his life?"

"Well...I..." I stare into the amber liquid and blink. "I guess I made the decision for him," I mumble.

"Fucked up, babe. Totally fucked up."

I swallow half the glass before placing it on the bar, turning toward Tobias. "He doesn't know what he's in for. He only got a taste. I won't do to him what's been done to me."

"Ain't right." He shakes his head, judging me for my decision. "Every man should be able to make that choice. No one, not even his lady, should make it for him without at least a talk first."

"I've only known him for a few days."

Tobias blinks, gaping at me. "Wait. You've only known this guy for a few days, and you're stewing over him like you've lost the love of your life."

"Well...yeah, but..."

"There's always a but," he utters, running his palm over his beard and across his mouth. "Women always have buts."

"You ever meet someone, and you just click?"

"Yeah. A few times a week, at least."

I roll my eyes.

"I ain't about love, babe."

"Jo," I correct him.

"Ain't about love, Jo. I've had my heart broken once, never doing that shit again. I'm a one-and-done kind of guy."

"Nick is the kindest and most maddening bossy man I've ever met, and I've known some pretty bossy fuckers back in LA."

"LA is filled with pricks."

"That shit is the truth," I laugh, smiling at Tobias.

"So, you met a guy, instantly fell for him, and now you're running away because..."

"My life is too complicated for him to handle."

"He feel the same way about you?" Tobias asks before taking a slug of the beer he's been nursing since he sat down.

"I don't know," I mutter with a shrug. "I think so. His mom made me soup today."

"You've known him for a few days, and you've met his mom—or, wait." Tobias pauses, sliding the beer back on the bar top. "Does he live with his mom?"

I scrunch my nose. "No, he has his own place. I wasn't feeling well, so he called her, and she made me homemade soup."

"Yeah, you fucked up." His eyes narrow. "Super fucked up."

"Tobias, you're not helping."

"When a man calls his mom and brings her into the circle, introducing her to any woman...that means something."

"I was sick, and he was being nice."

"No man is that nice. You fuck him?" Tobias asks point-blank, and I don't even flinch at his candor.

"No."

Tobias rocks back. "Guy didn't even get inside you yet, and he's already staking his claim, showing you off to his mom. That right there is some heavy shit."

"That's not how it works."

Tobias leans back in the chair, laughing. "Babe," he mutters.

I always hated that word...until Nick. He was the

only one I liked who called me babe. The only person who ever said it in a way that made my chest flutter and my belly roll.

"You fucked up because that's exactly how it works. I know shit's different in LA, but here in the South, when you bring together the family and a woman, that means something deep and heavy."

"He doesn't know who I am, though."

"You a killer?"

I laugh and roll my eyes. "No."

"Stalker?"

"No."

"Thief?"

"No."

He taps the hair hanging where his chin should be. "Rapist?"

"What?" I jerk my head back. "No."

"What the fuck is there to know?" he asks, shrugging a shoulder. "Guy found himself a beautiful woman, kind of normal in the head but with the right amount of crazy."

I narrow my eyes at his assessment of me. I'm completely normal. Well, at least I am compared to the other people around me in LA.

"Killer rack. Long legs. Pretty mouth. Beautiful eyes. Probably a sweet heart too, but also a total pain in the ass nonetheless. And yet, he still wants that. But the first chance, she takes off, stealing that decision from him. That's some fucked-up shit."

"It's not. He'll never be able to understand because we come from two different worlds," I tell Tobias, never able to fully explain the fucked-upness of my life to someone from the outside.

"You from Mars?"

"No."

"Mercury?"

"No." I roll my eyes.

"Earth?"

"Yes, Tobias, I'm from Earth."

"Same world, babe. Same fuckin' world. Just because you think it's different in your head doesn't make it reality. I know men get a lot of shit, but we're pretty damn resilient. He should at least get a say in what he wants before you yank all your sweetness away from him. You fucked up. Fucked up big."

"Yes, she did, Tobias." Nick's voice is unmistakable, and so is the anger in his tone.

"Nicky," Tobias greets, turning his body and reaching his hand out to him. "How the fuck you been, man? It's been a hot minute."

Nick takes his hand, shaking it, but his eyes are completely focused on me. "I was good until I met this chick and she ran away like her ass was on fire before I had a chance to talk to her."

Tobias's eyes slide to me and then back to Nick as their hands drift apart. "Ah. I was running out of shit to say, man. Didn't think you were ever going to get here."

Nick shakes his head. "Fuckin' traffic, Tob. Sorry, bro."

"No prob. You introduced her to Angel, dude? That's some pretty heavy shit."

"Does everybody know everybody around here?" I mumble under my breath, earning a glare from both men. Fuckin' great.

"I see she spilled her whole life story to you already. Must be nice to share something with a complete stranger that you can't share with me."

Tobias puts up his hands, sliding off the stool. "This is some nutty shit. I think I'm going to let you two work it out alone. Nice to see you again, buddy."

"Thanks, Tobias. Stop by the shop sometime soon and say hi. I'm sure Tam and Mammoth would love to see you."

Tobias smiles, showing those white teeth from behind his beard. "Love the fuck out of those two."

Tobias isn't gone for more than a few seconds when Nick stretches out his arms on either side of me, his hands resting palm down on the bar top. "No more running, babe." The hardness of his chest presses into my back as his warm breath skids across the skin of my neck. "It's time to talk. No more bullshit. No more lies. We're about to get very real."

13

NICK

"Don't be mad at me," she begs, not turning her head to meet my gaze.

"Babe, way beyond mad. You took off. No explanation. No hesitation. Left. Poof. Gone."

"I'm sorry," she says in a softer, even more hushed tone, her head tipped down, staring at her lap.

I lean closer, almost resting my lips against her ear. "Why run? I was going to take care of the guy, making sure whatever was going on wasn't going to blow back on you. You didn't give me that chance, though, before you set off, not even bothering to look back."

"I looked," she argues.

"When was that? Before or after you ended up at this shit-ass bar?" My thumb brushes against her pinkie, and the same electric shock I felt when I touched her before zaps me again.

"I tried to leave. Tried to drive away. I figured it was

better for you. Easier, even," she explains, tipping her head toward me, causing my lips to press softly against her ear. "But I couldn't. Jesus, I couldn't. It's why I'm at this shit-ass bar in the middle of fucking nowhere, spilling my guts to a biker named Tobias, instead of lounging at the beach or boarding a plane."

"You weren't leaving?" I whisper into her ear, moving my hands over hers, my arms pressing against her exposed skin.

"No." She turns her head until my mouth is next to her lips instead of her ear. "I tried, but it's like you have an invisible tether, holding me back, keeping me from moving forward." She lifts her fingers, intertwining them with mine. "I've only known you for a short time. This shouldn't be so hard. But you don't deserve the shitstorm that's about to rain down on you because of what happened earlier."

"The photos?" I ask, staring into her blue eyes, seeing the sadness and remorse buried deep inside them.

"Yeah," she breathes, smelling of sweet whiskey.

"I don't give a fuck about photos, Jo. The only way I give two shits is if the photos are going to cause problems for you. I have nothing to hide. Some asshole posting photos of us kissing isn't going to cause that much trouble in my life."

Her eyes flash with anger. "You have no idea what it's like, Nick. I'm not a simple girl. I come with baggage. Way more baggage than anyone you've probably ever met. That single second, the one damn snapshot, will change your world forever."

I slide my hand up her arm until my hand is at her neck, resting my thumb on her cheek. "Do you think I give a single fuck what anyone thinks about me?"

"No," she admits, her eyes locked on mine. "I don't think you do."

"Will it ruin you?"

"Hopefully." She smiles softly.

"You lookin' for a little trouble, babe? Want to drive a wedge between your past and your future?"

"I want out. The last few days have been..." She swallows, pausing for only a moment as I keep my eyes on her, not moving a muscle. "The best I've ever had."

Grim.

It's the only way I can describe whatever her life has been if the last few days have been the best she's ever had. She's attempted sleeping in a parking lot, gotten drunk and ended up kneeling on my bathroom floor, and had a massive hangover. I don't know of too many people who put those things on any best experience lists.

"That's fucked up," I mutter, my gaze dipping toward her mouth as her tongue slides out, sweeping across her upper lip.

"I know."

"Come home with me," I tell her, not one hundred percent understanding why I'm working so hard to keep around a girl I've just met.

I've never chased, always sitting back, waiting for

them to do whatever they wanted. But then again, I never had someone stick around for more than a fuck before showing them the door and helping them right out.

Jo's eyebrows rise. "You still want me? Even after I ran?"

My fingers tighten around the back of her neck as I pull her face toward mine until our lips are touching. "I don't think I've ever wanted somebody more," I admit against her mouth, being as truthful with her as I am with myself, even if I don't understand the why of it either.

She shifts her entire body to the side, and she slides her arm around my waist as I take her lips hard and fast. Diving my tongue deep, I breathe in her whiskey-scented moans, taking what she has to give without remorse.

She pulls back, taking her soft lips with her. "Take me home," she pleads between labored breaths.

"No more running."

"No more running," she promises.

Keeping our hands locked, I toss a twenty on the bar and help her from the stool. Before we get too far, I swing my arm around her shoulder, stalking toward the door.

Tobias catches my eye, raising a glass in the air, lifting his chin in approval. I return the gesture, not stopping for a talk or a thank-you. Whatever he did or said kept her here long enough for me to get here.

When we hit the parking lot, Jo starts moving toward her car, but I pull her back by the waist. "Leave it. We'll get it tomorrow. You've been drinking, and you're not driving. The last thing we need is you pulled over for suspicion of DUI."

She turns to me with pursed lips. "I'm not drunk, Nicky."

"You may not be, but the smell of whiskey coming off you is more than enough to at least get a breathalyzer, and although my dad is ex-law enforcement, the last thing I want to deal with is a cop right now. We'll swing by and grab it tomorrow."

"You're the boss," she mutters.

I smile, unable to stop myself. "You're learning." I open my truck door, helping her inside. "Last chance to finish taking that run, leaving me and all this in your past."

She looks around, then back at me, her gaze sweeping across my face. "I'm done running. There's nowhere I'd rather be than right here with you."

My chest tightens at her words, and I grunt my approval, not trusting my voice enough to speak. I seal her inside, move to my side of the truck, and take off toward home.

14

JO

We're within a mile of his house when my phone rings, but I ignore it, instantly sending the call to voice mail.

Kimberly.

She's going to chew my ear off or maybe my ass out for the photos that have no doubt been leaked already.

"You should probably answer that." Nick glances toward me, his eyes flickering to my phone.

"I don't want to." The words are barely out of my mouth when the phone starts again.

Kimberly's relentless. It's why I hired her as my PR person five years ago, needing a pit bull on my side instead of relying on my parents' people to have my best interests at heart.

I sigh, tapping the *answer call* button. "Hello." I swallow, instantly regretting listening to him.

"I've been calling you for two hours. Where the hell have you been?" she bites out.

"Around." I peer over at Nick and grimace.

"The photos are everywhere. You're failing at lying low."

"I know. I'm sorry. I was, but then—"

"The guy is *freaking* hot, by the way," she says so loud that even though she's not on speakerphone, I know he heard every word because Kimberly is never soft-spoken.

Nick turns his head, his eyes on me, smile on his face.

I bite my lip as my face heats. "Kimberly..."

"Well, I'm only saying. He's, like, way hot. Freakishly hot."

"You've now used freak twice within thirty seconds." I turn my body toward the side window and away from Nick. "He's right here. Can we talk about this later?"

"Don't stop on my account," Nick teases behind me.

"He's right there?" she asks.

"Um, I said that. He's next to me."

"Put me on speakerphone," she demands.

"No."

"Yes," she pleads.

I sigh. "Fine," I snap, pressing the button on the screen so we can both hear her. "You're on speaker now."

"Good. Hey there, handsome. I'm Kimberly, Jo's publicist. You two have caused quite a stir."

"Already?" he says, shifting in his seat and sitting up a little straighter.

"Yep. Hard not to when you two have your hands all

over each other like two horny teenagers. It's not often a Hollywood starlet is found being groped by a greased-up hottie outside the circle."

I give him a sorrowful smile. "Sorry."

"I've fielded a few calls, and I'm sure they're digging into your background. Anything I should know so I can start a plan of attack?"

He turns his head, staring at me as we sit at the stoplight. "A plan of attack for what?"

"For whatever skeletons you have hanging in that closet of yours. We all have something to hide, some more than others, and it's my job to crush those bones or make sure they're at least downplayed enough that the dirt never gets disturbed deep enough for them to be found."

His eyebrows draw in, and his face darkens. "For fuck's sake."

"Sorry."

"Babe," he says in that cool, sweet way that's grown on me faster than I could have ever imagined. "Don't be sorry. Ain't your problem. It's mine."

"So, there are skeletons?" Kimberly asks.

"Not many, but I'm sure they'll find the few I have."

"I need details," Kimberly demands, followed by the sound of papers moving. "Let me find a pen."

"It's not that long of a list," he tells her, gripping the steering wheel harder and pulling himself closer to the windshield.

"Well, I don't want to forget something that may be critical. Okay, I'm ready. Hit me with the worst of it."

"I was sent to boarding school at fifteen," he admits, looking out the windshield as we move through the intersection.

Boarding school? He doesn't seem like any boarding school kid I've ever met. They were always so prim and proper, being molded for greatness and greed. I would've bet my entire fortune he'd gone to public school, staying close to home.

"Why?" she asks.

"I was a little wild."

I laugh, finding those words completely believable. There's nothing about him that says boring or even rule-follower. Maybe that's why I like him as much as I do. I've spent my life trying to play by the rules and follow the status quo, when all I wanted to do was break free, spread my wings, and experience freedoms only regular people seemed to enjoy.

"I stole a car with my buddies. Pop wasn't happy about that shit since he was ex-DEA. He had a fit. Said I was out of control and needed to learn something more than he could teach me. He was grooming me to follow in his footsteps, maybe join the military even, but I wasn't about that life and set out to do whatever I had to do in order to make sure those choices were impossible."

I blink, soaking all that in because it is a lot. So much information to unpack there. First, his father was DEA and worked for the government. Second, Nick wanted to make sure he couldn't be pushed into the same position or follow the same path as his father. Third, he stole a car.

Freaking stole someone's ride and was caught. That's the big thing. His *pop* would not have sent him to boarding school if he didn't know, and the only way he'd find out was if Nick were arrested.

"Was that the only time you were arrested?" Kimberly asks.

"No, but it was the first."

I blink again, my mouth falling open. "Serve any time?"

"Not that time. My pop got me out with a few phone calls, but the next day, my ass was sitting in the headmaster's office at the most conservative military boarding school in the state."

"And that school would be?"

"Andrews Academy."

"Graduate from there?"

"No."

"Why?"

My eyes widen, and I can't stop myself from staring at him in disbelief. He'd stirred up all this shit, but you wouldn't know it from the way his mom talks to him and about him. She adores her son, never uttered a bad word about him to me in the brief amount of time we spent together. She gushed over him like any normal doting mother. Never said anything about his past indiscretions.

"I was making and selling fake IDs. One kid got caught, he ratted me out, and I was tossed out on my ass double time."

"What year?"

"Senior."

"Damn," I reply. "Your parents had to be so pissed."

"Dad was for a hot minute, but he got over it, and we moved on."

"Still close with your parents?" Kimberly asks.

"Yes."

"Arrested for the fake IDs?"

"No."

"What other arrests?"

"B&E at twenty."

I blink, full-on gawking at him. "What?"

He shrugs like it's nothing. "I lost a bet. Had to follow through on that shit, but they set me up and sent the cops for shits and giggles."

"Serve time for that?"

"Nope."

"Dad?" she asks.

"Yeah," he sighs. "Man pulled my ass out of more fires than I deserved."

"You own part of the automotive repair shop?"

"It's not a repair shop," he corrects her.

"Are you part owner?"

"I own a third. My cousin and her husband own the other parts."

"How did you pay for your share?" she asks, keeping up the rapid-fire questions at a breakneck pace.

"Trust fund from family inheritance. Every kid in my family gets a million bucks when they turn twenty-one."

"What?" I gape.

"Old-school family money." He shrugs, glancing my way. "I bought my house and the business with it, but I have a little left over in case I ever need it."

"Any of that money gained through illegal means? I know you're Ita—"

"Don't say it. I don't like people talking shit about my family because we're Italian. None of that money was obtained through any illegal means. The money was made through the sale of a business our family owned back in Italy."

"But everyone has that kind of money and still works?" I ask before Kimberly has a chance to ask another question.

"A million bucks doesn't go a long way, babe. And anyway, no one in our family sits on our asses. I don't care if they have ten mil in the bank, we're not sitting around in our underwear, napping all day, and shitting away our lives. We all own businesses or at least have a career. A strong work ethic is instilled in us at an early age."

I knew plenty of rich kids. Hell, I was one myself. Money gained through no work of our own, but many people didn't bother to lift a finger or find any way to be a productive citizen besides shopping so much we could prop up the economy of some small countries with our annual spend.

"So, no mob ties?"

Nick grimaces. "I have a great uncle, my grandpa's brother, in Chicago, who served federal time for some shit."

"This is going to be interesting," Kimberly mutters. "Anything else?"

"Nope."

"Crazy ex-girlfriends?" she asks.

"No ex-girlfriends. I don't date."

I can't stop the frown hanging from my lips.

No ex-girlfriends? No matter what someone says, I always assume they're full of shit. Who makes it to their mid-twenties, never having a long-term relationship? No one I know, even if they only lasted a few months. But Nick is dead serious.

"Well, kids, this is going to be a bumpy ride. I hope you're prepared for what's already in motion," Kimberly tells us. "Jo's already been through shit like this, but, Nick, for you, this will all be new."

"Whatever. It is what it is, Kim."

"Kimberly," she corrects him.

"Kimberly," he mutters, shaking his head. "What can we do to make shit go away quicker?"

She sighs. "Let me come up with a plan of attack, and I'll get back to you in the morning."

"Works for me," he says, pulling into his driveway. "What about you, babe? You got anything you want to say or add?" He says those words while staring at me, leaning against the door of his truck, looking so damn good, I want to sink my teeth into him.

"Um, not really." I shrug, feeling the ache between my legs from the smoldering look he's giving me.

"Shit," Kimberly hisses. "Your mom is calling me."

“Damn,” I mutter. “I’m turning off my phone. Handle her.”

“It’s why you pay me the big bucks, babe.” She throws that in, knowing how I felt about that word in the beginning, but not knowing how much it’s grown on me.

“Thanks, babe,” I toss back at her.

“Later.”

“Bye,” I say to her, tapping the screen before glancing back at Nick. “I’m so sorry. So, so, so, so sorry.”

The words are barely out of my mouth before he’s across the truck, pinning my back to the door, his lips on mine, kissing me hard and breathless.

15

NICK

We're barely inside the door when Jo's on me, legs wrapped around my body, lips covering my mouth. Her body fits mine perfectly, pressing against me in all the right places, leaving no space between us.

"I want you," she begs against my mouth, digging her fingers into my hair and holding me to her. "I need you."

I have my hands on her ass, pinning her back against the wall, wanting her as badly as she needs me. "I want you too," I tell her, moving my mouth away from hers.

The skin on her neck is soft as I slide my lips down her body to the swells of her breasts peeking out from her tank top. Her hands never leave my hair as she grinds against me, riding my fully clothed cock. Using the wall for support, I use one hand to pull down the strap of her tank, exposing her black lace bra, which doesn't leave much to the imagination.

I peer up at her, and her eyes are on me, pupils

dilated, breath heavy and rushed. "Don't stop," she pleads, and I've never been one to disappoint.

When I release my hold, she slides down my body, and for a moment, a frown appears on her lips. As soon as I reach for the bottom of her tank top, her lips tip up and her hands immediately move to my T-shirt. We're tearing at each other's clothes, stripping away each piece of material one by one and tossing them to the floor.

I only spend a moment staring at her completely naked, but the sight is magnificent. Her pale skin is flawless underneath all that clothing. Her blond hair spills over her shoulders, stopping above her breasts. Her figure is classic hourglass, but not rail-thin like most celebrities.

Her eyes drink me in at the same time. Her appraisal of me is slower and more methodical, while mine is scattershot. First, she stares at my chest, something she's seen before because of my aversion to wearing a shirt when I'm home, preferring to be in as little clothing as possible. Her look can only be described as greedy, but when her eyes drop farther, they widen.

"Holy fuck," she croaks. "Is that a..."

"Yep." I smirk, moving my dick so she can see the metal piercing.

"I've never..." She moves her hand to the skin below her neck as her fingernails slide back and forth over the top of her breasts.

"Don't worry, baby, it won't hurt," I promise her.

She licks her lips, gawking. "I'm not worried about that. I only wonder if it'll feel—"

I cut her off, charging toward her, lifting her into my arms. "It'll feel fucking fantastic," I murmur against her skin, peppering her body with kisses.

She winds her legs around my body, pressing her pussy against my cock. She digs her fingers into my hair again, lifting my lips back to her mouth and away from her breasts. "Go slow with me," she asks. "I want to savor this moment."

"Babe, if I only last a moment, we have a problem."

She laughs softly as I move us toward the bedroom, preferring to explore her body in a different position. Her mouth never leaves mine as we move through the house, her pussy rubbing against my dick in the most agonizing fashion with each passing step.

Once inside my bedroom, I lean over, pressing her into the mattress and placing myself on top. When I back away, her eyes are soft, her lips plump and red, and her chest is rising and falling at a rapid pace, almost panting.

Crawling down her body, I wrap my fingers around her ankle, yanking her ass to the end of the bed in one quick move. She squeals, shocked by the speed at which I moved and the ease with which her body followed. Before she can protest, using my hands, I spread her legs, pressing my lips to the soft skin of her lower thigh right above her knee.

She giggles at first, trying to close her legs, smashing my head a little, but it doesn't stop me. Wrapping my hands around her legs, I hold them open, wanting to spend time worshiping her body, tasting every drop she has to give.

Her legs fall open the farther up my mouth moves. I peer up her body, keeping my eyes on her the entire time. When her hand moves to her breast, pulling at her pert nipple, fingering the tip and moaning, I almost lose all control.

I growl against her skin, trying to stay calm and ignore the ache between my legs. This is about her. Making her feel good, bringing her to the brink of orgasm, only to pull back and give her my cock instead.

My mouth slides up her legs, moving to her pussy, kissing her flesh whisper-soft until she squirms against my face. I go with her movements, covering her middle with my mouth, lavishing her body with my tongue.

She moans, tweaking her nipple harder, gripping the sheet with her other hand. Every time my tongue comes close to her clit, she twitches, gasping and seizing like she's never had someone touch her in the way I am.

Her body's sensitive and her clit even more so, needing the lightest of touches to elicit a major response. Moving slowly and softly, I circle her clit with my tongue, closing my mouth around the spot that makes her stop breathing.

"Nicky," she says in the sultriest tone.

I lift up, my lips covered in her wetness and my spit, loving the fuck out of eating pussy, especially hers. "Yeah, baby?"

"I want your cock."

Who am I not to give a woman what she wants? It's not my place to judge or question, only to please. Climbing up her body, I reach over and open the nightstand, fishing out a condom. She watches me closely as I rip open the wrapper using my teeth, her fingers still at her nipple, tugging lightly.

"You're driving me fucking wild with that," I tell her, kneeling between her legs, sliding the condom down my rock-hard shaft.

"I need to come," she pleads, her eyes pinned on my dick, but I ain't mad about it either.

"Hard or soft?" I ask her.

"Hard and fast," she tells me, placing her feet flat on the mattress, lifting her bottom off the bed. "Hard and soft."

I suck in a breath, trying to keep my shit together long enough to make this worthwhile for both of us. I don't remember the last time I was this worked up over any chick, but here I am, lusting after a woman I barely know, but somehow feel like I've known forever.

I lean forward, holding myself up on one arm, moving my other hand between her legs, finding her wet and not from my mouth. When I push a finger inside, her mouth falls open and her eyes flutter closed. Her wet warmth coats my fingers, milking them with each thrust inside her. My mouth finds her lips, swallowing her moans and pleas for more.

A second later, my hand is gone, and my cock is at her opening, pushing inside her at a slow and agonizing pace.

This isn't love.

This is lust.

Pure and simple, unadulterated need.

She curls into me as soon as my cock is fully seated deep inside her. Her mouth at my ear, nibbling her way down my neck as her fingernails dig into my back. The mix of pleasure and pain drives me forward as I pull out, thrusting my cock back into her in one solid movement, without hesitation and faster than before.

Our tongues twist, tangling around each other as our bodies move together. Me thrusting, her pushing, fucking each other's brains out like we've never had cock or pussy before.

It's hot. Sexy. Carnal.

I don't know how long we stay like this, but my thighs burn until the moment her body grows still and she chants my name like we are at a concert and I am the headliner.

"Fuck," I moan, following her over the cliff, pumping into her a few final times as the pleasure takes over, stripping everything, including my breath, out of me.

Her body goes still and slack underneath me, her hands still on my back, but her nails no longer piercing my skin. "Jesus," she murmurs, her eyes glazed over like she is drunk again. But this time, it is from my dick and not from a cheap-ass drink. "That was..."

"Fuckin' amazing," I say, suddenly finding the air again.

"Yeah..." She blushes underneath me, staring up at me like I rocked her world.

That wasn't even a good performance. It was rushed, but I was horny and needed a release, and she didn't seem like she was in the mood to take it slow either.

I lean forward, kissing her lips, gentle this time, almost thanking her for the gift she's given me. "Be back," I tell her, climbing off the bed with unsteady legs, stalking toward the bathroom.

I peer over my shoulder, finding her eyeing my ass, watching my every movement. She smiles when I catch her staring, and I know I have her. She's not done with me, not ready to run away again, not ready to head back to Hollywood until she's at least had her fill of me.

I pause, my hand about to grab the filled condom, thinking about the fact that my life is here and hers is there.

What the fuck is wrong with me?

I don't even know what the hell I'm thinking about anymore. Was Mammoth right? Is there more between us than just friends who clearly have benefits? I've never run after a woman before, but I chased her down, using every avenue available to me to find her.

After I throw the condom away, I place my hands on the edge of the sink and stare at myself in the mirror.

Do I have feelings for Jo?

I can't deny the pull.

Is it love?

Besides my family, I'd never loved another human

being before. Not in the way a woman should be loved. But things with Jo are different.

I have a need to protect her, loving to see the easy smile on her face instead of the look of dread or sadness I saw the first time I laid eyes on her.

"Nicky," she calls out after a few minutes. "You okay? Did I do something wrong?"

I close my eyes, hating that she questions herself, always placing blame in her lap, even when she's done nothing wrong.

Her mother has done a number on her. "Coming, babe. Washing up," I yell back, knowing I can't stay in here all night.

Our relationship is what it is. If she wants to be with me, wants to explore whatever this is, I'll go with it, letting her into my world like I've never done with anyone else.

But can you love someone after only a few days? Possibly.

I've never introduced a girl to my mother or my entire family, but I've already done one of those with Jo, and tomorrow she's about to meet the entire gang.

If this isn't love or at least heading in that direction, I'm not sure I've ever felt the same immediate pull toward another human.

Do I only feel this way because she seems wounded and in need of rescue? I probably wouldn't have given her the time of day otherwise. But it isn't where my feelings for her come from.

"Come back to bed," she begs from the other room. "Or do you want me to go to the couch?"

I take a deep breath, knowing I need to make her feel comfortable and know she's no longer a guest in my home. I want her here. I want her in my bed. I want to roll over in the morning and smell her perfume on the pillows and catch a whiff of her on my clothes all day when the wind blows in the right direction.

A moment later, I'm back in the bedroom, taking the empty spot next to her, sliding my arm under her back, and forcing her body to curl into mine. "I want you right here."

She peers up at me, her pale skin against my olive. "Are you sure? I mean, I could—"

"No, babe. You're right where you belong."

Her smile is easy and quick. "I feel at home here." She places her hand over my heart, resting her palm between my pecs. "For the first time in my life, I feel like I belong somewhere I never thought I'd be."

My heart stutters underneath her touch and because of her words. It's never felt so right having someone in my arms.

Not until now.

Not until her.

"I like you right where you are, babe. Made to be there."

She lifts her head, staring up at my eyes with her deep blues. "Made to be here?"

"Made to be here," I repeat.

"I'm worried," she admits with a small frown. "I'm worried this is all some amazing dream, and everything's about to come crashing down, including whatever this is we have growing."

I brush my fingers against her back, stroking her soft, porcelain skin. "Babe, you enjoy the ride, feel the safety, and let me worry about stopping anything from ruining what we're building."

My words must do the trick because her frown vanishes, and her face softens again. "I can do that," she says, lying back down next to me, curling into me, her head on my shoulder, hand on my heart.

Mammoth was right.

I am whipped.

In a short amount of time, a woman has gotten me by the balls first, the heart next, and I'm not sure I will ever be able to let her go.

She snuggles deeper into me, closing her eyes. "Night, Nicky."

"Night, sweetheart," I murmur, brushing my lips against her forehead.

I close my eyes and know I'm fucked.

16

JO

I GLANCE AROUND, MY EYES WIDE. "HOLY SHIT. There're so many cars and bikes here."

"It's Sunday dinner," Nick tells me from the front of his bike while I clutch his middle like I still have a chance of falling off and killing myself.

"When you said family dinner, I don't know why I thought it would be your parents, grandparents, and us."

Nick laughs, his body shaking in my arms. "Babe, family means the *entire* family. Sundays are always at my grandparents', with everyone in attendance if you're in town. And there's no if, ands, or but about that, or my grandmother will lay into the missing party."

"But there're like twenty people here," I mutter, still in total disbelief with a heavy dash of shock.

"More than that." He taps my legs. A simple gesture without using words to tell me it is time to let go and climb off. "Don't freak out."

My feet are on the ground a moment later, but my mouth is still hanging open at the craziness of what they have. "I still can't believe the entire family is here. Maybe I should..." I back away. No freaking idea where I'm going, but this seems like an important event and nowhere I should be.

"Stop," he snaps, reading my thoughts without my having to share my doubts. "I see that wild look in your eyes, like you're about to bolt. There's nowhere to go, babe. No reason to run for the hills."

I glance down, kicking at a stone near my feet. "I don't know what I'm walking into here. We never had family anything at my house. If there was a party, it was all my parents' friends or people in the industry. There was nothing intimate about it. This feels more..."

He hooks me around the waist, hauling me back until I'm between his legs and his face is nuzzled in my neck. "Babe, what we did last night was intimate," he says, nibbling on the sensitive skin below my ear.

I shiver in his arms as my skin tingles everywhere.

When his hands grope my ass, squeezing, my knees almost give out, but he only tightens his hold on me.

"This is a fuckin' good time," he murmurs against my skin.

My fingers burrow in his hair, holding him against my neck, loving the way his lips move across my skin. "Are you sure you haven't brought any other women here?" I ask, always loving to torture or compare myself to the other women in his life.

"Never," he answers, his warm breath skidding across my flesh. "Only you, babe. Only you."

I smile, staring at the house, loving the hell out of the idea that I'm the first. Probably the only first I'll ever be able to have with him. "Why me?" I ask, more to myself than him, but I still say the words out loud.

"Do you want to know me?"

"Yeah."

"Want to understand what type of man I am?"

"I think I already do."

He shakes his head. "To know me, you have to know my family. Not only my mom, but everybody."

"Everybody?" I swallow.

He nods. "Every single person has played a role in making me who I am today."

"Maybe this is too soon," I offer.

"It's not too soon. They won't even bat an eyelash about you being here. There are too many people to keep track of everyone. You'll blend right in. Half of them won't even notice you're there."

Why do I feel like that's a lie? Blend isn't something I've ever been able to do. Even when far away from my element, I stick out like a sore thumb. I did my best today, wearing a T-shirt and jeans I'd packed for the plane ride, when I'd usually throw on a ball cap to do everything possible to hide my identity.

"Are you sure?"

"One hundred percent," he assures me, taking my hand and leading me toward the house.

"This place is beautiful." I scan the exterior, taking in the pristine house with not a bush or flower out of place, impeccably manicured and well taken care of.

"My grandparents have lived here since before I was born."

I don't know how it feels to live in one place for too long. My mother moved around a lot, always jumping to a bigger house, having to show off for the others who worked around her in Hollywood. Nothing said status like a grotesquely large home with more rooms than most small-town hotels.

My feet slow as we get closer, and Nick squeezes my hand. "Don't be nervous, babe. Think of them as guests at a party, and if that doesn't work, picture them naked. It's what I always do when I get nervous."

I laugh, finding it hard to believe that Nick ever gets nervous. He always seems perfectly comfortable in his skin, no matter where he is or who he's with. "I can't picture your family naked."

"I couldn't do it." He grimaces. "But you can. Whatever makes you not lock up and turn mute. My family is going to love you."

My feet stop moving entirely, and I yank him back enough to stop his forward momentum. "But what if they don't?"

The words are barely out of my mouth when the door swings open, and there's an older woman with sleek, straight gray hair filling the doorway. "Nicky," she greets, her eyes bright and her smile wide. "My boy."

"Nana," he says, moving forward, taking me with him since our hands are still connected. Using one arm, he hugs her and leans in, kissing her cheek. "I've missed you."

"My sweet, beautiful boy, it's been a week. You don't need to butter me up with your nonsense," she teases, smiling at him.

He laughs, and I cover my mouth with one hand, trying not to be heard, preferring to be invisible.

"Where's the girl?" she asks.

My eyes widen, and my laughter dies a quick, swift death.

Nick steps to the side, outing me to his nana.

Her smile grows larger as her eyes sweep over me, soaking me in, studying my every physical feature. "Always knew you'd settle down with a blonde."

I choke on my own spit, going into a major coughing fit.

Nick shakes his head, but there's a smile on his face. "Nana, behave. Jo and I are..."

"Don't lie to me, Nicholas. You've never lied to me, so don't start now." She steps out onto the walkway, and he moves farther to the side, leaving me totally exposed.

I don't know what to do. I stand there, frozen, scared, wondering if I should run. Nick said they're all nice, but maybe it was a lie. Maybe his version of nice is different from mine. And how would he know how they'd treat me since I am the first woman he's ever brought to his family's Sunday dinner.

"I'm Nana," she offers, her face bright and cheery. "You can call me Nana too, or Grandma, but nothing else."

"Yes, ma'am," I reply.

She raises an eyebrow, and her smile disappears.

"Nana," I correct myself quickly, never wanting to disappoint her for some reason, even though we've only just met.

"Good girl," she says, touching my arms, still studying me. "You're more beautiful than your photographs, my sweet dear."

I smile nervously. "Thank you," I say, but the tone sounds more like a question.

"I can see why Nicky's so smitten with you. A classic beauty. He's not into these done-up floozies around here. He needs a good girl like you."

"Well, I..." I swing my gaze toward him, hoping for a rescue, but he doesn't give me one. "I don't know if I'm—"

"Nonsense. My grandson has always had a wild side. Since the day he was born, he had a wild hair up his ass. He needs himself a good woman to ground him."

Nick tips his head back, staring up at the sky. "I'll never live shit down."

"Come. Everyone's waiting to meet you," she pleads, pulling me toward the house.

I narrow my eyes at Nick as I pass by. "I thought you said they wouldn't notice me."

"I lied," he laughs. "But don't worry, they're harmless."

"Traitor," I mutter before putting on my brightest smile and following his grandmother into the house.

There are so many people, I'm almost in shock. Can he really be related to everyone here? And do they really come here every Sunday to sit down to eat and catch up? My mother has thrown smaller cocktail parties in LA, intimate affairs for friends and coworkers, but never anything for our family. The fact that they wouldn't speak to her was the issue. No one wanted to be around us unless there was a financial reason for being in one another's lives.

Nick's mom is the first person who steps forward with a dark-haired and olive-skinned man who is an older version of Nick. "Jo, I'm so happy you're feeling better today. This is Thomas, Nick's father and my husband." She says these words while hugging me, taking me away from Nick's nana.

"It's so nice to meet you, sir," I say, trying to speak as Angel gives me such a big hug, she almost makes it impossible to breathe.

Thomas's eyes move over my face, studying me like he can see into my soul with a simple glance. "It's a pleasure to meet you, Ms. Carmichael."

Nick is the spitting image of his father. Same serious and cocky attitude, along with an appraising look that can make a fully clothed person feel completely naked.

"Jo, please," I tell him, noticing the fine lines near his eyes and the smattering of gray hair near his temples.

"Jo," he corrects himself. "I'm glad Nicky was able to find you yesterday before—"

Angel smacks him in the chest and moves in front of him. "Don't get overwhelmed. It's easy with so many people, but remember, they're all pulling for you."

"Pulling for me?" I repeat to her as Nick and his father talk quietly behind her.

"They're excited to meet Nick's first girlfriend."

I swallow, knowing the magnitude of today, but girlfriend... Am I? Are we more than casual acquaintances who had sex? Feelings are there and are undeniable. The spark was instant, and the promise of something more smolders underneath the surface.

"Breathe, and if you feel overwhelmed, come find me," she says, touching my shoulder when I don't reply. "Breathe, Jo."

I inhale deeply, trying to right myself as I see more people coming my way. Behind them is the crew from the bar the other night. Tamara, Gigi, Lily, Mammoth, Pike, and Jett. They're sitting around a table with two empty seats, hopefully saved for us.

Angel takes my hand, moving me toward a large group of people. "I don't expect you to remember anyone, so smile and nod your head."

"Okay," I say, glancing back toward Nick as he gives me a chin lift, letting me go.

The men in the family are all beautiful, wide chests, broad shoulders, muscled up for their age, and the ink is even more impressive. They don't look like anyone I know in Hollywood, but their handsomeness would make them fit right in. "These are Nick's uncles. This is Joe," she says, pointing to a man who could make any woman weak in the knees. "Mike, Anthony, and Nick's aunt Izzy."

Izzy is the first to move forward and grab me, pulling me in for a hug. "Finally, another woman around here, and a beautiful one at that."

"Thank you," I offer, not sure what else to say. "You're pretty damn gorgeous too."

I feel awkward, and I'm used to people looking at me all the time, living under a microscope in California or in the shadow of my mother's beauty and success.

Izzy's long brown hair is pulled back in a tight pony, slick on the sides without a strand out of place. "This is my husband, James, and those—" she points to two boys and a teenager across the room "—are my sons Carmello, Rocco, and the youngest is Trace."

Her husband is freaking sexy with an air of danger, and her two oldest sons no doubt inherited the traits from their father.

Everywhere I look, I see handsome men and beautiful women, but that shouldn't be surprising, given Nick's good looks. If these people are anything to go off of, Nick's going to get better looking with age and not require the same plastic surgery regimen many older people in my life in California seem to follow on a regular basis.

"Is there something in the water here?" I ask myself, but Izzy overhears, smiling at me.

"Good genes and happiness, Jo. Stress and unease will age a person quicker than years. Life's to be enjoyed. Savored, even. It doesn't hurt when you have someone you love who's hot as hell too. You know?"

I laugh softly, nodding. "If your family is anything to go by, I'd say you're the happiest people on the planet."

"With good genes," she adds, giving me a wink. "But yes, I'm happy, even if my husband tries my every nerve and he's now taught our sons to do the same. Do you see my gray hair?" She leans in, turning her head to show me the side of her head, pointing to the silver streaks. "These are because of the four males in my household. They're trying to age me, and so far, they're winning."

"Don't listen to her," James, her husband, insists, coming to stand next to her and sliding his arm around her waist in a sexy, possessive way. "She does it to herself. Our boys are exactly who they were meant to be, and they love their mother more than anything in the world."

She peers up at him as he glances down, their looks smoldering and hot. "They can love me and age me at the same time."

"We're getting older, baby. Can't stop that, but I gotta say, you're getting sexier with age."

She wrinkles her nose. "I refuse to get old."

He laughs, brushing his lips against her temple. "We're getting older together, and there's no one else I'd rather have at my side than you."

I swoon a little for this man I barely know. The way he looks at his longtime wife makes my heart sing and part of me a little jealous. I want a shared history, years in the making with another person. I want someone who's going to look at me with nothing but love after decades together.

Nick's suddenly next to me, his arm snaking around me in the same possessive way James has done with Izzy. "Hey, Uncle." He gives James a quick chin lift. "How's work?"

"Your father is keeping us busy as always."

"You two need to retire someday." Izzy rests her head against her husband's chest.

"When are you going to retire, my love?" he replies, tangling his fingers in her hair.

"My work isn't dangerous."

James laughs. "Your answer is a non-answer. You've perfected deflection."

"I perfected it long before you entered my life, sweetie," she replies, smiling.

"Make way," a small woman proclaims, carrying her phone. "Old lady coming through."

James moves Izzy to the side, his arm still around her waist and a hand resting on her hip as the woman gets closer.

Nick leans over, bringing his mouth next to my ear. "She's Fran. She's a wild old lady, but harmless. Be happy you're not a guy."

"Why?" I watch as the woman who's dressed like

she's ready for a starring role in a classic rock video gets closer.

"Because she has a thing for younger, muscular men, and she loves to make her husband jealous."

"And her husband is?" I ask.

Nick points across the room to an extra burly man covered in tattoos with a long gray beard and hawkish eyes. "She does whatever she can to get a rise out of him. It's their foreplay."

When the woman, Fran, stops in front of me, she grabs my hands, and her gaze moves up and down my body. "Damn, she's a looker," she says sweetly. "You did good, Nicky."

Nick laughs, squeezing my side. "Thanks, Aunt Fran."

"Bear, baby, come meet Jo!" she yells over her shoulder to her husband, whose eyes haven't left her body since the moment she walked away from him.

He grumbles, mumbling to himself, and makes his way through the crowd and across the room.

"He's mine," she spouts as if I'm going to do something to try to steal him.

"You're a lucky woman," I tell her, but I'm being honest. He's a little rough around the edges, but he's still handsome. The man is big, and I'm thinking the size carries everywhere on his body too.

"Hey, Jo," the man says, his voice sweet, smooth, and low. "It's a pleasure to finally meet Nick's girl."

"I'm not..."

"Bear, behave. Jo and I are only friends."

Bear stares at him, not blinking, no smile. "Keep lying to yourself, Nicky boy."

"He's not wrong," I agree. "We're friends."

"You two do the horizontal mambo yet?" Fran asks point-blank.

"Um, we..." I bite down on my lip and stop myself from answering. Sex isn't something we talk about openly in my family, not that I've ever wanted to with my mother or father anyway.

"Fran," Bear chides her. "Class, baby."

"Fine," Fran says, looking from him to me. "Bear and I started out as friends too, but the way Nick's holding you doesn't say buddies."

I don't move away, liking the way he's holding me. And what she says is true. No friend of mine, not even my closest, has ever held me in the same possessive way he does...but I like it.

"We're exploring our options," I say, figuring it is an answer that will satisfy all parties involved.

"Exploring is half the fun." Fran winks. "Am I right?"

"Aunt Fran, you're incorrigible."

She reaches out, tapping Nick's cheek lightly with her hand. "I may be old, sweetie, but I'm not dead. Live life to the fullest. Live it hard and fast, because someday, you'll be old and hurt yourself sleeping."

"What?" he asks as she pulls her hand back.

"You'll understand when you're older."

"Fran, leave the kids alone. Let them live in oblivion."

"Here's the man of the hour," Fran says, her eyes moving over my shoulder at the sound of footsteps.

"My grandpa," Nick whispers in my ear. "But don't make a mistake. He's not in charge. This family is not a patriarchy. My grandma holds all the cards and is one hundred percent the boss."

"All the women are the bosses," Fran tells him, shaking her head. "The men need the illusion of control just like they enjoy a pair of fake breasts, but there's reality and fiction."

"What?" I wonder.

"Ignore her. She talks in riddles and sometimes doesn't make sense, but I think she likes it that way," Nick warns me.

"Nicky, my boy," Nick's grandfather says, walking up to us. "I see you've been busy this week."

Nick reaches up, rubbing the back of his neck. "You saw the photos, huh, Grandpa?"

"I did. Who hasn't? But," he says, his eyes moving to me, though not in a judgmental way, "none of that matters as long as you two are happy. I'm Sal." He holds out his hand toward me, and I slide my palm against his. In one swift and elegant motion, he pulls my hand to his lips, placing a soft kiss on my skin. "It's a pleasure to meet you, Josephine."

The way he says my name makes it sound like the most beautiful word in the world. There are hints of Nick in his features and motions, and it's like looking into a mirror at Nick's future self.

"You too, sir," I reply as he straightens but keeps a hold of my hand.

"Sal, please." He smiles, and my insides go all soft, not from attraction, but from his simple act of kindness and the sweetness in his tone.

"I'm sorry about any unwarranted attention my presence in Nick's life has brought on the family."

Sal shakes his head. "We can't control everything in life, Josephine. You two did nothing wrong, and there's no need for you to apologize because someone wants to make a big deal out of a kiss between two consenting adults. Just know when you're here, around my family as part of this group, you're safe and we've got your back."

I blink, soaking in what he said. No one has ever had my back unless they were on my or my family's payroll. Understanding what it means to be loved and cared for unconditionally and without financial incentive is something that would take me more than a little while to get used to.

"Girl, get your butt over here!" Tamara yells out, waving her hand high in the air and pointing toward the open chair next to her.

"Go," Nick's grandfather orders. "I hope you don't mind sitting at the kids' table."

I laugh, thinking he's joking. "Thank you, sir."

"Sal," he corrects.

"Sal." I nod.

"He ain't lying," Nick mutters as we move away from Sal, Fran, and Bear.

"People really do that? I thought that was all television nonsense."

Nick laughs, squeezing my side again. "You have so much reality to catch up on, babe. So much reality."

And I am about to get a heavy dose.

17

NICK

"Take this home," Nana says to Jo, handing her a giant container of spaghetti and meatballs. "I want to make sure you have enough to eat."

"Nana," I say, shaking my head. "I do know how to cook."

Nana turns her eyes to me and smiles. "I know, baby, but it doesn't hurt to have leftovers. You two look like you could use a few extra carbs."

I roll my eyes, and Jo laughs. "You're ridiculous."

"Baby-making uses a lot of calories," Nana adds.

Jo starts to choke, pounding on her chest with one hand, and twists her head, trying not to look at either of us.

"I can't believe you said that," I mutter under my breath, taking the container of pasta from Jo so she doesn't drop it.

"Wishful thinking," Nana replies, giving me a devilish smile. "A grandma can dream."

I slide my arm around Jo, holding on to her. "Ignore my grandmother. She sometimes goes off the reservation."

"I do not," Nana argues, crossing her arms. "I'm throwing things out there into the universe, hoping they come true."

"Marie," Grandpa says, coming to stand next to her, his eyes moving from me to Jo and back to his wife. "What did you say?"

"Babies," I tell him. "She's always talking about babies."

"Are you two pregnant?" Grandpa asks, clearly having had too much wine and not enough food today.

"Oh my God. No. We've known each other like three days."

"But you could be?" he asks, raising an eyebrow.

I shake my head, laughing at the insanity. "We have to go," I tell them because I can't stand here listening to them and all their baby talk with a woman I just met, who isn't even sure she likes me all that much. "We have to get home to—"

"Make babies," Grandma adds, finishing my sentence.

I move us toward the door, keeping Jo close and under my arm. "I'm so sorry," I say to her as we step outside before the door has a chance to close.

She peers up, smiling at me, tears in her eyes from her

coughing fit. "They're great. Really great, Nick. You're so lucky."

"You only say that because you don't have to put up with their craziness all the time."

"I'd take their fun crazy over my mother's totally insane, snotty, passive-aggressive anger."

"Is she really that bad?" I ask.

Jo stops and turns toward me when we make it to my bike. "She's probably worse than I can even describe. After watching your family and all the love they have for one another, my mother is more like a supervillain. She's not lovable in any way."

"Somehow she made you, though." I lean forward, pressing my lips to her forehead and place the pasta on the roof of my cousin's car.

She closes her eyes, soaking in my touch. "My nanny made me who I am, not my mother, Nick."

"That's so sad, babe. Makes my heart hurt for ya."

She wraps her arms around me, resting her head against my chest. "I wonder what my life would've been like if I had a family like yours. Christmases and birthdays have to be so much fun and filled with nothing but happiness."

"Damn, not even a nice Christmas?"

"My mother's an atheist and won't celebrate even if it's the retail version of the traditionally religious holiday. We never had a tree, never saw Santa Claus, and I never once had a stocking hanging from a mantel."

"Babe," I mutter against her hair, feeling my chest

ache imagining what it had to be like for a little blond-haired girl like her, growing up with no holiday cheer. "You missed out on so many wonderful things. We have to change that."

"Nick." She curls her fingers into the back of my T-shirt. "Maybe someday I'll have all the things I missed out on, but stop acting like it's your problem to make my life something it's never been."

I pull back, touching her chin with my two fingers, forcing her to look at me. "You're right, Jo. It's not my problem, but I'll be damned if I'm going to let your life continue to be shit. You're with me now, in my world. And my girl, in my world, gets what she wants. You want a Christmas with all the trimmings? You want a tree, ornaments, Santa, stockings, gifts, and more? I'm going to be the man to make that happen, no matter what I have to do to make it your reality."

"Nick," she whispers, but I don't let her say anything more.

"Get your sweet ass on the bike, babe. We got shit to do."

"What shit?" she asks, blinking at me.

"It's time to shop."

An hour later, after switching out the bike for my truck and putting the spaghetti in the fridge, we're parked outside a year-round Christmas shop, and Jo has her nose almost pinned against the windshield. "What the what?" Her mouth hangs open as she stares at the gaudy and way overdone decorations. "Is this for real?"

I smile, loving the surprise on her face. "Yeah, babe. It's real. I have a few decorations at home, but I want you to pick out some of your own. We're about to do some major damage."

"Major damage?" she gulps, turning her eyes to me. "Now?"

I nod.

"It's August."

"Don't give two fucks. My girl wants Christmas. I'm giving her Christmas."

"You're a little crazy."

"Only for you." I climb out of the truck, rounding the back, and open her door. "Normal is way overrated and completely boring. Think you can handle this?"

She nods, sliding her hand in mine, letting me help her from the truck. "Are you sure about this?" she asks, peering to the left and at the giant blow-up Santa Claus that's waving to all the passersby.

"Never been so sure about anything in my life."

We walk toward the store, my fingers intertwined with hers as she glances around, not sure what to look at first. "This is overwhelming."

"We'll take our time. Get whatever you want."

"Whatever I want?"

"Yep. You want a ton of pink shit to match your cute little suitcase, then we get all the pink shit they got."

She smiles, her face all soft and sweet. "Who are you?"

"I'm the guy who's going to give you the Christmas you never had."

"You don't need to do this to make me happy."

"I do."

She shakes her head. "You don't, though. You've already made me happier in a few days than anyone else has in my entire life."

"That's some sad shit, Jo."

I usher us into the store, done arguing about what I should or should not do. The one thing I know is I always do whatever I want, and there's nothing I want to do more than see my girl smile. She lights up a room when she's happy, and based on everything she's said, she wasn't all that happy before she ended up in my world.

"You know this is insane, right?" she asks as we step inside to the sound of Christmas carols and the whistle of the Christmas Express moving above our heads.

"Do you like this?" I motion toward the room where Christmas exploded, vomiting happiness everywhere.

"Happier than I've been in longer than I can remember."

"Then I love this. Now," I say, patting her ass, moving her forward. "Get that fine ass moving because we have a house to decorate."

Jo steps back, gaping at the ten-foot tree covered in pink and white ornaments and the brightest white lights

I've ever seen. "Have you ever seen anything more beautiful?" she asks me.

I stare at her, seeing the joy on her face, the lights twinkling in her blue eyes. "Never," I reply, but I'm not talking about the tree.

Jo turns toward me, face tipped up from looking at the tree. "Nick, I'm talking about the tree."

I reach up, placing my hand at her neck, unable to take my eyes away from her mouth. "I know, but I'm not."

"Why are you so good to me?"

I don't have an answer. At least not an easy one or something that makes any semblance of sense outside the tiny bubble we've created in a short amount of time. So, being who I am, I answer the only way I know how.

I bend my head down, taking her mouth soft at first until she opens to me, and then I kiss her deep, hard, and demanding. My hands find her ass, squeezing her cheeks tight, curling my fingers around the plumpness.

Her hands are in my hair, pulling hard enough to cause a rippling sensation to travel down my spine, creating a direct link to my growing cock. Tonight isn't supposed to be about sex. Everything is supposed to be about Christmas, but I can't stop myself in the faint glow of the tree and with the happiness on her face at something so simple I've taken for granted my entire life.

"Thank you," she murmurs against my lips, staring at me with our faces so close, there's an intimacy to it I'm not sure I've ever felt before.

"Tomorrow, we do presents."

"Presents?" she gasps as her eyes widen.

"Lots of presents," I tell her. "If we're going to do this, we're going to do it right."

The doorbell rings, pulling us out of the moment.

"Are you expecting someone?" she asks, no longer staring into my eyes but moving her gaze toward the door.

"No. They can fuck right off."

"You can't not answer the door," she says, trying to wriggle out of my hold.

"Fuckin' A. There are no rules about answering a door, especially when someone isn't invited over. The only person I want to see is standing here with their fine ass in my hands and their lips wet from my kiss."

The doorbell rings again and again in quick succession, followed by a loud pounding.

"Sounds important."

"Nothing is more important than this," I tell her, still not moving to answer whoever is bothering us at this time of night. "Nothing good ever happens at this hour around here."

"Nick," Jo says when the pounding grows louder and whoever is on the other side isn't taking the hint. "Open it so we can get on with our night."

I sigh, releasing my hold on her, and move toward the small table in the dining room. I reach inside a drawer, pulling out my Glock 43 because I have a feeling whoever's on the other side isn't a friendly face.

"Oh my God. You have a gun?" Jo gasps, her eyes wide and pinned on my Glock.

"Babe. It's the South in the middle of fucking nowhere. Everyone has a gun."

Her eyes only widen, and I know my words didn't give her solace, but sometimes, the truth is the best answer and the simplest.

"What?" I ask, gun down at my side as I pull open the door, ready for anything.

A tall woman, wearing high heels, a slim-fitting dress, and sunglasses is standing at my door, with a sleek black limo running at the curb behind her. "Where's my daughter?" she asks, her head tipping down toward my hand. "Have you taken her hostage?"

Madeline Carmichael. I've never seen one of her films, but the wealth and snobbery ooze off of her.

"Mother?" Jo gasps, walking up behind me but not moving in front of me. "What the hell are you doing here?"

"Has this man been holding you against your will?" her mother asks her, ignoring me.

"God, no. Don't be ridiculous."

"He has a weapon, Josephine. What kind of man answers the door with a gun in his hand?"

"What kind of man doesn't do what he needs to do in order to protect what's his?" I ask, hating her asshole attitude already.

Madeline pushes past me, walking into my house and grabbing her daughter by the arm. "Get your shit. We're leaving."

"No," Jo barks. "I'm not going anywhere."

"Don't you dare talk back to me, child."

Jo pulls her arm free from Madeline's grip. "Mother, I'm a grown woman. I'm not your child, and I'm not sure you've ever truly been my mother. You may have given birth to me, but besides that, when have you ever cared enough to come fetch me?"

Madeline removes her sunglasses, folding them slowly and way too calmly. Her back is perfectly straight, years of impeccable posture on full display. "Have you seen the photos and headlines?"

"No," Jo snaps and moves toward me, winding her arm around my back as I lift mine over her shoulder.

Her mother's eyes follow her daughter's movements and then turn to me, narrowing. "You're dragging our family name through the mud for some redneck hillbilly who brandishes a weapon when he opens the door and has a Christmas tree up in his house in the middle of summer, for Christ's sake. You are coming home with me and putting this behind you. You'll be returning to Jamison and doing everything possible to repair the damage you've caused. You've had your time in the gutter, girl, but now it's time to grow the fuck up and come back to reality."

Jo's fingers dig into my sides, and her body stiffens. "No, Mother. I won't be coming home with you, and I most certainly will not be getting back with Jamison. I don't care about my reputation—or yours, for that matter. The last few days have been the happiest of my life."

"With this...this redneck?"

"I thought I was a hillbilly?" I ask, being sarcastic as fuck because who the hell does this woman think she is?

"You're clearly lower class, no matter how cute and quaint your house is," Madeline taunts, looking down her nose at me.

"Mother," Jo chides her. "Stop being rude. Nick has been nothing but kind and treated me like a normal person for once."

Madeline laughs and shakes her head. "He's after your money, sweetheart. Nothing more. You have nothing else, besides what's between your legs, a man like him could want. He has nothing to offer you. No future. Nothing but shame. You've both done enough damage, and it will take years to repair. Get your shit. We're going. The plane takes off in an hour."

"No." Jo curls into me, tethering her body to mine with her hands. "I'm not leaving."

"You childish, spoiled bitch," Madeline spits, stepping toward Jo.

I move in front, pushing Jo behind me. "Lady, I don't know you, and I give zero fucks who you are or how much money you have. The one thing I know is you don't walk into my home and talk shit about my girl. I don't care if you gave birth to her or not, you do not talk to her that way. Say whatever you want about me, I can take it, especially from elite trash like you. But once you call her names, threaten her, or try to boss her around like she's property, we have a problem. And right now, we have a big problem."

Madeline huffs, tipping her chin upward. "You're not a member of this family."

"Family?" I ask, laughing. "I don't see a family. I see a self-serving mother trying to force her adult daughter to do something against her will, and in my world, that doesn't fly. So, you can either see yourself out or I'll put you out, but you're not staying here, and Jo is not leaving with you."

"Josephine," Madeline hisses. "You're going to let him talk to me this way?"

Jo's hands are at my sides, fingers curled into my shirt, and her face is buried in my back. "Go, Mother. I don't want you here. I don't want you anywhere in my life."

Madeline's gaze turns lethal. "You're nothing without me."

Jo moves slightly, peeking her head around my body. "I was nothing with you or to you, Mother. But here, I feel like someone. I feel like I can finally be me. Just go. Leave us be. I don't want to be in your world anymore."

"You think the paparazzi is going to leave you alone? You're still my blood, and they'll do anything they can to embarrass me."

"You do enough to embarrass yourself," Jo tells her mother, causing my eyebrows to rise. "Between Dad's affairs and your shitty behavior toward every person in your life, you have no problem making it into the news rags on a daily basis. If I stay here, away from you and out of LA, they'll leave too."

"Delusional," Madeline mutters. "I should have you committed."

With those words, I gently grab Madeline by the arm, careful not to hurt her, and hustle her toward the door. "It's time to go, ma'am. You've said enough. Don't step foot on my property again, or I'll have you arrested for trespassing."

She tears her arm from my grasp. "Get your hands off me, you filthy beast. I should have you arrested for assault."

I laugh. "Try it, lady. I know every cop within a hundred miles. Ain't no one going to do shit to me. But by all means, try it. Knock yourself out. I'm sure the papers will have a field day when they get their hands on the story."

With one final huff and a grunt, she stomps out the door. "This is your last—"

Jo reaches around me, slamming the door shut in her mother's face. "I'm so sorry," she says immediately, falling against my chest and into my arms as soon as I turn around.

"Baby," I murmur, running my fingers down along her hair and kissing the top of her head. "Don't be sorry. You didn't do anything."

Her body shakes, but she's otherwise silent. No doubt she's crying over the vile and inexcusable things her mother said while standing in my living room.

"Your mother doesn't deserve you," I tell her, holding her tight, letting her get her feelings out.

"She's an awful person, Nick. So awful."

"She is," I say softly, giving her time to deal with whatever shit is going through her head. "But you need to know, you're nothing like her and you're special, babe. So damn special, the sun shines a little brighter with you around."

"Nick," Jo whispers, tipping her head back to look at me.

I lift a hand, wiping away her tears. "You deserve the world, Josephine, and as long as you'll let me, I'm going to do everything in my power to give it to you."

18

JO

NICK AND I SPENT THE NIGHT ON THE COUCH, staring at the twinkling lights of the Christmas tree. After the scene my mother caused earlier, Nick's embrace and the decorations calmed my frayed nerves.

"Morning, babe," he says, his voice like gravel coming from deep inside him as I lie there with my head on his chest.

"Morning." I trace the lines and ridges of his abdomen. "You sleep okay?"

He slides his hand up and down my arm, warming the skin cooled by the air conditioning. "Better than ever."

"Lies," I tell him, smiling as I stare at the delicate ornaments he let me pick out in every shade of pink.

On the next swipe of his hands, he stops near my hair, toying with the ends of a few strands. "You know what today is, right?"

"Um..." I pause, thinking about it, knowing it's Monday, so maybe work for him and boredom for me. "Not really," I admit.

"Christmas present shopping."

I gasp, sitting up in the crook of his arm, digging my elbow into the couch and turning my face toward him. "We're shopping?"

His laughter is deep and delicious. "Babe, never saw you so excited. Guess I know what makes you tick."

I smile, my face flushing. "I don't live to shop, but I do love a good store."

"Gotta remember this isn't Cali. There's no Rodeo Drive around here, but we'll make do with the few shopping malls nearby."

"I don't need the fancy stores," I lie because although I don't need them, they're like a fantasyland of wonderful and pretty things. "Wherever you want to go."

"Rural King?"

I scrunch my nose. "Rural what?"

"Rural King. It's an amazing store, and they literally have everything you could ever want."

"Shoes?" I ask, raising an eyebrow.

"Yep. Crocs and boots."

I stare at him funny, pursing my lips. "That's a negative, big guy."

He pulls me down with his hand on the back of my neck, planting a kiss on my cheek. "The mall, it is. But first, we eat."

His morning stubble tickles my skin as I smile. "I

hope you don't think I'm going to make breakfast unless you're in the mood for cereal."

Nick laughs softly and releases me. "We're going out to this little diner in town, and then we'll shop till you drop."

"Nicky, I could shop for hours," I tease, winking.

"There are a lot of women in my family. I have no delusions about your ability."

I chuckle, pushing myself up, untangling my legs from his. "I can be ready in an hour," I tell him, climbing over his body.

He swats my ass before I make it all the way off the couch. "Make it thirty. I'm starving."

As soon as my feet touch the floor, I turn, placing my hands on my hips. "This takes more than thirty minutes."

"Hey." He reaches for my hand and pulls me closer. "Are you okay?"

"Yeah. Why?"

He squeezes my fingers, giving me a sorrowful smile. "About what happened last night. Your mom..."

I hold up my hand, having spent enough of my life worrying about her and her feelings. "She was being exactly who she is. I'm surprised she took time out of her busy life to fly across the country and demand my return, but other than that, it's just the same old, same old, Nicky."

His lips flatten. "No one should have to deal with a mom like that. I'm so sorry."

I shake my head, giving his hand a squeeze back.

"Don't be. There's nothing I can do to change what's happened in my life, but I can make my future whatever I want it to be, and she won't be a part of it."

"And your dad?" he asks.

"He's not as judgmental, but he couldn't care less about me. I hear from him at the holidays and whenever he's in town to negotiate a new movie, only because his agent requires him to attend in person. Other than that, he's not in my life."

Nick sits up, his fingers still intertwined with mine. "Do you like it here?" he asks me, his face serious, eyes focused on mine, and pulls me between his legs. "Being here with me?"

I peer down at his handsome face and the soft, kind look he often has when he's being sweet instead of a hard-ass. "I like being here," I admit honestly. "It's nice to be myself without worrying about anything or anybody."

He opens his mouth, but I place my finger over his lips. "Plus, you're not hard on the eyes, and I feel safe with you."

He smirks. "I make you feel safe?"

"Of course." I run my fingers through his messy bed head. "No one has ever stood up to my mother like you did last night. No one has ever had my back, Nick. You grew up with a family who loves you and would do anything if you asked. I never had that. Never until I met you, but I know we're only—"

This time, he shakes his head, interrupting me. "Don't say we're only friends, babe. It's more than that. I know it. You know it. Can't lie to ourselves about whatever this is." He takes my hand and places it against his chest over his heart. "You feel it, don't you?"

"I do," I admit. "And it scares me."

"Scared enough to run away?"

I shake my head and swallow, finding the words stuck for a moment. "No. I'm not going anywhere. Not until I know."

He scoots forward, wrapping his arms around my legs, and I leave my hand on his chest. "Know what?" he asks, and I can feel his heart picking up speed with every word.

"If this is what I think it is." I drop my hand, tangling my fingers back in his dark hair.

"And you think it is?" He lifts my shirt, placing his lips near my belly button, making my insides flip.

"I can't say, or I'll jinx it."

He lifts his gaze to me, lips still against my skin. "You don't believe in jinxes, do you?"

"I don't know what I believe anymore."

My statement is completely honest. Within a few days, my life has been turned upside down. What I always thought was real isn't anymore. The neatly crafted façade of Hollywood has vanished, and it no longer looks as shiny as it has my entire life.

Spending time with Nick and then his family, I crave something more. Something real. Something more like them, his family.

Am I in love with Nick?

I don't know, but I know we are heading that way.

I've had more feelings for him in a few short days than I've ever had with any man I've dated before. He's treated me better, cared for me, cooked for me, and done everything in his power to please me without expecting anything in return.

Is Nick in love with me? I don't know that either. I'm sure he feels the same as I do, wanting to see where this is going to go.

"I turned your world upside down," he says with a smug grin, sweeping his fingers across the skin at the back of my legs.

It takes everything in me not to react to his soft touch and throw myself at him. "Something like that."

"You want me," he taunts, peering up at me with his blue eyes. "Admit it."

I can't contain my laughter. Not because he's lying, but he's so damn honest all the time, even when it comes to calling me on my bullshit. "Can't lie, baby," I say sweetly, tamping down my giggles. "I do have a thing for you and your pretty face."

"My girl has a thing for me," he repeats, his smile growing wider.

The way he says *my girl* has my belly fluttering and my heart racing like I've sprinted down the driveway, chasing after something uncatchable.

"I think every woman has a thing for you."

He leans forward, pressing those soft lips to my skin again. "They don't matter. Only you."

The warmth of his breath scatters across my flesh, and I squeeze my legs together out of instinct and need. The memory of how his lips feel and the pleasure they can deliver is not forgotten, especially by my body.

I push away, needing an escape and a shower before we let this go any further and accomplish exactly nothing today except pleasure and orgasms.

Before he has a chance to reach for me and haul me back between his legs, my phone rings at his side. He glances down, staring at the screen. "Kimberly's calling."

I sigh and roll my eyes. "She's never a good call this early in the morning. It's not even six in LA."

He lifts the phone, hovering his finger over the screen. "Want me to take it?"

I snatch it from his hand before he has a chance to answer the call. "No. No. I'll take it," I say to him, moving toward the bathroom.

"Still thirty minutes," he yells out. "This man needs food for what we're about to do today."

I'm hoping he has more than shopping on the agenda. While I could shop for hours, I don't want to do that today. I'm planning on more time with Nick nuzzled between my legs and exploring his body too.

"Mornin', sunshine," Kimberly says as soon as I answer the call.

"Morning, darling. What has you awake at this hour?" I ask in a chipper voice, putting up a good front because I know she's about to drop a doozy or at least chew me a new one.

"Your wretched mother," she mutters, followed by a yawn. "She called me late last night and told me I needed to reel you in. She's going on a daytime talk show today, and she knows they're going to ask about you and your escapades in Florida."

"I don't care what she says, Kimberly. She showed up here last night."

Kimberly gasps. "In Florida?"

"Yep," I say, pulling open my makeup bag, opting to do my makeup before showering. Not the best order to do things, but the only way I can possibly be ready in time. "She showed up at Nick's door, demanding I leave with her, spouting all kinds of Madeline Carmichael attitude."

"Damn," she quips.

"It wasn't pretty."

"But you didn't go?"

I grab my concealer, starting on my eyes because they look like I haven't slept in days. The dark circles underneath always become more pronounced during times of stress, and holy shitballs, my life has been a hot mess. Except Nick. He has been my only saving grace. "No. Nick pushed her out the door, and I slammed it right in her face."

"No way."

"Way."

"You're shitting me."

"I am not shitting you. Madeline was in the middle of a sentence, but whatever she had to say was said to the door and not to my face." I force the smile from my face to blend the concealer into the light foundation I've applied, careful not to mess it up and go over my thirty-minute time frame.

Kimberly laughs. "I'd have paid big money to see her face when that happened."

"I'm sure it wasn't pretty, but she deserved it."

"She's never been kind to you."

I sigh, knowing Kimberly's words are true. I've lied to myself a long time about my mother's behavior, forgiving her and assuming it was the typical mother-daughter bullshit. But at some point, I realized she treated me more like another prop in her collection than her child. "She sure as hell wasn't last night. After insulting Nick, she turned on me. He wasn't having any of it."

"Sounds like a keeper, babe," she teases. "And from what I can see in the photos the paparazzi have sold, he's fucking beautiful too. It's a win-win."

"You aren't mad?" I ask because I know she's going to give me a long answer, which will make applying my eye makeup easier.

"That you found yourself a hot and decent man who kisses you, holding your ass while he does it? Um, hell no. My job is your publicity, and right now, public opinion of you has never been better. Keep doing whatever you're doing, including that man. I'll handle any fallout from your mother, but I wanted you to be aware she is going to be on television today, promoting her next heart-wrenching blockbuster."

"Sadly, I'll have to miss her performance about being

a fabulous mother, juggling it all, including a daughter who refuses to follow in her mother's footsteps."

"Eh, fuck her. You know I hate her and always have."

"I do. Anyway, I have to go. Nick's taking me to breakfast and then shopping."

"Wait."

"What?"

"He's taking you shopping?" she asks, sounding every bit a Valley girl.

"We're Christmas shopping."

"Are you doing drugs?"

"No. Why?"

"Christmas? It's summer, Jo."

"He's determined to give me the Christmas I never had growing up."

"You're making him sound better and better. I'm kind of jealous of the way he's taken to you. All the guys here are so..."

"Fake and needy?" I ask, rolling my eyes. "I can't say I miss that part of Hollywood."

"When will you be back?"

"I don't know. I'm sick of living my life on a schedule. Do I have anything pressing?"

"Nothing for a few months, but I can change that."

"I'll consider it, but I think I'm looking to take a longer break and focus on me for a little while."

"You do you, babe. Doesn't matter to me, and I think this time will do you some good."

Kimberly doesn't care. She's not my agent. She runs

my publicity, which means she gets paid whether I'm working or not.

"I have to run. I'm late, and I badly need a shower."

"I have so many things I could say right now," Kimberly teases.

"Byeeeee."

"Wait, one more—"

"Talk later," I say, disconnecting the call because I don't want to know what the other thing is, nor do I feel like fielding any more questions about my mother, Nick, or myself.

"Babe." There's a knock at the door, and I freeze, already halfway out of my panties. "You fuckin' around or getting ready? I hear a whole lotta chatting and not much showering."

"Stop being a creeper," I yell back. "I'm getting in now."

"You want help scrubbing your back?"

I think about the proposition for a minute, pausing with my underwear in one hand, hanging near my ankle. But I know a quick scrub will turn into way more, and then we'll be late, he'll be starving, and we'll have literally fucked away an entire day. Not that that would be a bad thing, but I had my heart set on Christmas and then cock.

"I'm good." My voice doesn't convince me, and I'm sure it doesn't convince him either.

"If you change your mind, you can join me in the guest shower. There's always room for you."

"Thank you," I tell him, finishing undressing.

"Fifteen minutes," he calls out before the sound of his footsteps grows faint.

I turn on the water, dancing in place with the cold air conditioning blowing on my bare skin. When the water finally warms up, I step inside, careful not to get my hair wet.

I wash away the bad memories of last night. The vile things my mother said. The pinched expression on her face. The way she looked down at me with such hatred and anger.

None of that matters anymore.

Today, I'm having Nick's and my very first Christmas.

19

NICK

"Where are you two going?" Gigi asks, walking into the diner as we are about to walk out.

"Christmas shopping," Jo answers without a second thought, and I instantly close my eyes.

Telling Gigi you're going shopping is an open invitation because, just like every other woman in my family, she can spend cash without even blinking.

"Christmas?" Gigi's eyes move left and then right, like we're the most insane people she's ever been around.

"Yeah," I tell her, taking a deep breath and then sighing. "Jo has never celebrated Christmas."

"Fuck, seriously?" she asks, her mouth hanging open. "Never?"

Jo shakes her head. "Never, but Nicky's going to change that," she says, smiling at me.

"Well, a girl can't Christmas shop alone or with the person she's buying gifts for. I'm off today." Gigi smiles, waggling her sculpted brown eyebrows. "You know, if you want to have a girls' day and get away from him," she offers, glancing at me, "for a little while."

"Well," Jo says, turning her face toward me, and I shrug, because I'm not the boss of her, and she can do whatever she wants. "I think…"

"Babe," I interrupt, squeezing her waist. "You do whatever you want. You want a girls' day filled with whatever a girls' day is filled with, you have a girls' day. I ain't gonna lie, shopping isn't my favorite, but I was doing it for you."

Jo's lips turn down along with her eyebrows. "I thought we were both buying things at the mall… No?"

I smirk. "I know where to go and what I'm getting you, and I can't get it at some luxury store that sells thousand-dollar shoes."

"Are you going to that King store?" she asks me.

Gigi's eyes widen. "Oh. My. God. You are not shopping for this girl at the Rural King."

I shake my head and lie my ass off. "Of course not. What kind of guy do you think I am?" I ask, placing my hand on my chest.

Gigi crosses her arms, cocking her head. "A dumb-ass one."

Pike grins, swinging his arm around Gigi's shoulders. "They have some solid shit there, though, darlin'."

Gigi twists her head so slowly it's like something straight out of a movie. There's no smile on her face or humor in her eyes. "You're shitting me, right?"

Pike shrugs, brushing his thumb against her bare shoulder. "I've bought you some gifts there."

"My boots for mudding and a rifle don't seem like things Jo would be super excited to receive as part of her first Christmas—or as a present, ever."

"But you loved your boots." Pike nuzzles her neck with his face.

She laughs, hunching her shoulders and squirming away from his lips. "I did, but I'm not Hollywood. I'm Floridian through and through, but I don't think Jo's ever been mudding a day in her life."

"Mudding?" Jo asks softly.

Gigi extends her hand toward Jo. "See? Not. A. Clue."

"Is it something I'd like?" Jo looks from Gigi to me.

"Babe." I laugh, pulling her closer and kissing her forehead. "A mudder, you are not."

"Bullshit," Gigi coughs. "We're so mudding. If your ass goes to Rural King, you get her boots and gear, but those can't be her only presents or I'm going to make you pay, Nicky."

"Fine. Fine," I grumble, even though I wasn't going to shop for her gift at Rural King anyway. But it was funny to see Gigi lose her shit over it.

"Good. We on, then?" Gigi asks Jo.

"If it's okay with Nick."

"Again, babe. You don't need my permission. Go, shop, and have fun. Pike and I will do our thing and meet back at the house later. Sound good?"

Jo curls into my side, wrapping both arms around my middle and planting a giant kiss on my neck. "This is going to be so much fun. Thank you."

"For what?" I grunt, staring down into her deep blue eyes.

"For all of this. The shopping. The friends. Christmas. Everything, Nick. Just everything."

"You haven't experienced a real Christmas unless you do one with the entire family. It's completely insane. Maybe you'll be around then, or if you're in LA, you can come back to celebrate with us," Gigi says.

The smile on Jo's face fades. "I'd like that," she replies softly, still clinging to me but talking to Gigi.

My chest aches, a totally unfamiliar feeling before Jo walked into my life but one that has now become commonplace. Every time the very words about her leaving pass through my mind, my body reacts and not in the good way.

"You ready?" Gigi asks.

I hold Jo a little tighter and press a hard kiss to her lips. "You have fun, babe."

"Are you going to miss me?" she asks out of nowhere like she's reading my mind.

"A little." I wink.

She smiles. "I'll miss you too."

"Oh boy," Pike mutters. "He's lost."

I glare in his direction, releasing Jo. "Don't go too far."

"Okay, Dad," Gigi says, pushing Jo toward the door

with one hand and holding up her middle finger with the other. "We'll be home by curfew, too."

"She's a pain in the ass," I tell Pike, shaking my head.

"She's my favorite pain in the ass."

"I hear ya and completely understand."

Pike tucks his hands in his pockets, glancing toward the floor for a second before bringing his green eyes back to me. "So, Jo..."

I hold up my hands, watching the women walk away through the glass of the diner door. "Don't say it, man. I know. I know. I'm so fucked," I whisper.

"Beyond fucked." He laughs. "Been there. Done that. Never the same."

"When did you know Gigi was the one?" I ask him, standing around talking about feelings like two chicks. But he is easier to talk to than Mammoth, who spends more time busting my balls than giving me actual advice.

"Spent a little less than a week with her, and I knew then I wanted more. But your cousin, in true Gigi fashion, took off, and I didn't see her for months." He shrugs. "She was almost out of my system when she walked back into my life, filled with attitude and venom. Knew right then I wasn't letting her get away again."

"So, like a week and you were a goner?"

"The heart's a funny thing. You know when the person isn't right, but when someone walks in and is supposed to be there, there's no denying the feelings, no matter how far or deep you push them down."

"Fuck," I hiss. "No one's gotten under my skin like her."

"Is it her or her celebrity?"

"It's her, Pike. It's her beautiful brokenness. She has this perfect façade, but underneath, she's missing so much. And I want to do nothing more than give her everything she's never had."

"Yep. You're fucked."

I shake my head with a wry smile. "Thanks for the pep talk."

"Well..." He takes a hand from his pocket, placing it on my shoulder as the women climb into Gigi's old Jeep. "The real question is, does she feel the same?"

"I need to get out of here," I tell him, getting too much in my feelings, something I've never done over anyone except my family.

I've spent my entire life shying away from relationships, doing everything possible to stop myself from falling in love. The one time I let my guard down and—*bam!*

I push past Pike and head outside, taking a deep breath and closing my eyes.

Shit.

What if she doesn't feel the same?

What if this is all a good time, and she is just living life on the other side of the tracks for a little while?

I'm sure I could and would get over her, but fuck, it would take for-fucking-ever, and I'd be a miserable asshole the entire time.

Three hours later, I am back at my place, surrounded by a pile of gifts for a girl I barely know but feel the need to show all the things she's been missing.

I haven't heard from Gigi or Jo in an hour, figuring they are knee-deep in girl shit or trying on so many shoes, Pike would have to build Gigi a new closet.

Me: Gigi, you guys almost done? Jo's gone MIA.

Three dots sit on my screen for longer than I expect and then stop.

Me: Hello...

Three dots pop up again, and I stare at my phone, waiting for an answer.

Gigi: I don't know where Jo is. I lost her somewhere.

My heart immediately starts to race, and my palms sweat.

Me: What do you mean, you lost her?

I pace the floor, back and forth in front of the Christmas tree we decorated last night, and dial Gigi.

"I don't know," she answers and before I have a chance to say anything. She's speaking so fast, she doesn't take a breath as she continues, "One minute she was there, and then she wasn't. I thought she wandered into a different part of the store, but I've looked everywhere, and she's gone. Poof."

The knot that has already settled in my stomach tightens. "Go to security, have them pull up the footage, and find her. I'm on my way."

"I'll have them look, but I'm sure she's here somewhere. Don't come. It's too far. There's no need to panic. I mean, I've lost Tamara a time or two here in the past."

"I said go to security, and I'm on my way," I tell her, my voice low as I say the words extra slowly. "Call me after they review the video footage."

"Okay," Gigi promises, not arguing with me anymore. "I'll do it."

I end the call and immediately dial my father. "Dad."

"Hey, kid. What's up? You doing good?" he asks, his voice filled with happiness which I'm about to crush.

"Jo's missing, Dad. She and Gigi went to the mall and—"

"I'm on it," he rumbles without even hesitating. "You headed there?"

"Yep." I stalk toward the door, only stopping to pull on my boots before heading toward my truck. "I have Gigi talking to security now."

"I'll do what I can on my end, but let me know as soon as you hear anything. Don't panic, Nick," he tells me in a calm and even tone. "I'm sure she's fine. You know how women are."

I skate right by that comment because if my mother heard him say that, I'm pretty damn sure he'd have a welt somewhere on his body. "Her mom was here last night."

"No shit. Why?"

"She showed up and told Jo she had to come home. It wasn't a request, but I escorted her out and let her know she wasn't welcome on my property."

"I'm sure it's a coincidence."

"Maybe," I begin, sliding into the seat before turning the key in the ignition. "Either way, I'm heading down there."

"I'll do whatever I can. I'll call when I have news, and call me when you know what the security footage shows."

"Will do," I promise, but he's gone before the last word is out of my mouth.

I peel out of the driveway, the trees and pavement passing in a blur as I head toward the highway and the mall in Tampa. I knew I should've gone with them, not leaving Jo and Gigi alone, especially with her celebrity status and the paparazzi searching for her.

"Fuck," I growl, slamming my palm against the steering wheel as I wait at a red light with the highway within sight.

The phone vibrates on the seat next to me.

Gigi: Here's a still shot from the video footage. She left with someone, but I don't know who he is. Photo coming.

I open the message, waiting, my eyes moving from the red light to the screen. A few seconds later, there's a shot of Jo with a tall, thin man holding her by the arm, moving her toward the door. The photo's grainy, but when I enlarge it...the man is unmistakable.

Jamison.

20

JO

"Let me go," I beg Jamison as he grips me by the arm, a gun in my back, pushing me toward the car. "Please. Don't do this."

He tightens his grip, digging the gun deeper into the ribs in my back. "Shut the fuck up. You brought this on yourself."

I walk faster, trying to move myself away from the gun, but it's pressed so hard against my back, it's useless. "Why are you doing this?"

"Why?" he asks, his voice filled with venom. "Why do you think?"

I'm careful to keep my head straight, but my eyes roam around the parking garage, looking for help. There's no one. The place is empty except for the luxury cars lining the rows. "I don't know, Jamison. I never did anything to you."

Can I talk my way out of this? He's never seemed

overly irrational, although he has a cruel streak when he's angry. Never in a million years would I ever think he'd be the type to wield a gun, especially at someone for any reason other than self-defense.

"You're a spoiled cunt," he spits, his fingers squeezing my upper arm so tight, he's cutting off the circulation. "And then you ran off with some common country gutter rat, leaving me as if I meant nothing to you and throwing away your life, our life, for some no-name man."

"I didn't leave you for him," I try to explain as I slow my steps, hoping to buy myself some time until someone is nearby and I can maybe get away.

"I wanted you back. I begged you to come back to me."

If there weren't a gun pointed at me, I'd laugh. He didn't beg me to come back. He demanded it and not by sweet-talking me either. Jamison Ryan never begs anyone for anything, especially women, and that includes me. "I'll come back. I wanted to come back," I lie.

"You did?" he asks, his voice quieter and softer for a moment.

"Yes." I curl my fingers into my palm, trying to hold myself together.

"Add lying bitch to the list of reasons why I'm here," he rages as soon as the words are out of my mouth.

My body jerks to a stop next to a blacked-out sedan. He keeps the gun pointed at my back but lets go of my arm, reaching for the handle.

I start to move and make it two steps, feeling freedom

is possibly in sight, when I'm hauled backward by my hair. "I should shoot you now and be done with you."

My neck cranes back, and I blink, trying to focus through the tears, and I spot the security camera above us. God, I hope someone's watching. Maybe they're coming, right? But they would've been here by now since our walk out of the store and to this point has taken more than a few minutes.

"You're hurting me," I wheeze, grabbing at his hands, trying to get them off me.

"You're lucky you're still breathing," he tells me, moving me back toward the car using my hair as a leash. "Get the fuck in."

I don't have a choice as he pushes down on my head, making my body fold into the seat.

"Hold out your hands," he commands, his dark eyes boring into me, lifeless and angry.

"I won't run," I lie again. "I promise."

"Your word means nothing to me, Josephine." He waves the gun in front of my face, making sure I remember who holds the power. "Hands."

Every minute I can stay alive is another minute Nick can find me. He'll find me, right? God, I hope Gigi noticed I disappeared and thought it odd, alerting Nick immediately.

I hold out my hands, letting the tears fall down my cheeks, giving in to the situation. I'm not giving up hope, but I have to play along long enough to be found.

Using only one hand, Jamison secures a pair of handcuffs around one wrist and the other to the door, making it impossible for me to run.

"I still don't understand why," I whisper to myself.

"Every brat needs a lesson," he tells me before slamming the door in my face and giving me a moment alone.

I keep my eyes trained on him, watching him round the front of the car as he takes in our surroundings. There's still no one around for it being the middle of the afternoon, and the parking garage is more than half full.

I yank at the handcuffs, wiggling my fingers around, trying to make my hand small enough to fit through the metal hole. My damn thumb is in the way, making it impossible for any crazy escape as he climbs in next to me, slamming his door louder than he did mine.

"There's nowhere to go, baby," he says in a salty-sweet tone. "You need an attitude adjustment, Josephine. Stop struggling, and this will all be over before you know it."

"Attitude adjustment?" I laugh bitterly. "That's priceless coming from you. You've always been a prick, Jamison. If one of us needs a new attitude, it's you."

But the last part of his sentence finally sinks is. *This will all be over before you know it.* Over? As in Jamison's going to kill me? Bile rises in my throat, and my body starts to shake enough for me to feel it but not enough for him to see.

I knew the possibility was there because he has a gun, but never did I think he'd actually kill me. I, in my dumbass reasoning, figured he was using it to control me, but that isn't his endgame at all.

Jamison is out for blood...my blood.

He stows the gun between his legs and lifts his hand to caress my cheek. "Always such a sharp tongue," he says, brushing his thumb against my lip, forcing my mouth open. "So soft and yet so sharp."

I want to gag at the way he stares at my mouth and the taste of his skin on my tongue. When he pushes the pad of his thumb a little deeper, I bite down. He lurches back, but his hand doesn't move. His thumb is pinned between my teeth as he howls.

But I didn't think this through, something I've been guilty of before, but never when my life was on the line. I only have one free hand, and the other is cuffed to the door with no way to run.

He reaches between his legs, fumbling for a minute, before lifting the gun toward my head. I smack it away, trying my best to keep ahold of his thumb and prevent him from pointing the gun anywhere else except my head.

"You fucking bitch," he screams, lifting his hand in the air and slamming the gun into the side of my head.

I cry out in pain, releasing his thumb as my vision blurs.

"You're going to pay for that," he says as the world around me goes dark.

"WHAT THE HELL DID YOU DO?" My mother's voice sounds distant and angry. "I told you to bring her to me, not beat her."

Heavy footsteps grow louder, moving quickly against hardwood. "She fought me, Madeline. What else was I supposed to do? You know how she is."

"Fuck, Jamison. Can you do anything right?" she hisses. "Now what? We can't have her like this."

"What are you saying?" he asks her.

"What do you *think* I'm saying?" she replies.

I keep my eyes closed, not moving, barely breathing.

Is she talking about...

No. She wouldn't.

She's my mother. She may be a bitch, but she wouldn't hurt me any more than I've already been hurt. Would she?

"You're the dumbass who used a gun, Jamison. I told you to bring her to me, but you took it upon yourself to go further than I ever imagined."

"Madeline, you said do whatever it takes. I did that."

"You're a fool. Go. I'll take care of her."

"Where am I supposed to go?" Jamison asks her, his feet no longer moving across the floor.

"I don't care. You're useless."

"You promised me a role in your upcoming film if I brought her to you, Madeline."

She laughs again, sounding more hysterical than sane. "You'll probably end up in jail after this...this stunt. I'll be lucky if I'm not in the cell next to you too. Jo is such a drama queen. I'm sure she'll go straight to the police when she wakes up."

I open one eye a crack, wide enough for me to see where I am. It's a room I've been in before, the suite Jamison and I had booked before he decided to enjoy a little more than the average maid service.

"Goddamn it. We can't let her do that," Jamison says. "Maybe we should..."

What the fuck?

I move quickly, taking off from the couch, heading toward the door since they're on the other side of the room. I make it within a few feet, lunging toward the handle when a hand comes around my waist and hauls me backward.

"Where do you think you're going?" Jamison grumbles in my ear as he lifts me off the floor, my legs kicking wildly. "The party isn't over, princess."

21

NICK

Jo's screams echo through the hallway as I run down the corridor toward the suite where I'd had my face-to-face with Jamison less than a week ago.

My dad and uncle are only a few minutes away, Pike and Mammoth are heading up in the elevator, having dropped everything when they heard what happened and where I was going.

As soon as I'm at the door, I lift my leg, kicking it open. Jo's in Jamison's arms, her legs swinging and kicking like a wild animal. Both of them swivel their heads around, and Jamison's eyes widen and then harden with hatred.

"Put her the fuck down," I order him, lifting the gun I have fully loaded, ready to put every bullet into him.

"Fuck you," he spouts, not releasing his hold on her.

Two shadows fill the doorway behind me as the first round of backup arrives.

"We can do this the easy way or the deadly way," I tell him, aiming straight for his head, knowing my aim is dead-on. I've been shooting since I was a little kid, my father finding the skill necessary even at that young an age.

"You won't shoot me with her in my arms."

"Do it," Jo tells me, tears trickling down her cheeks. "Shoot him, Nick!"

My gaze swings to the right as her mother moves into the room, dressed in a white suit, looking like class instead of the pure trash she is.

"Oh. If it isn't the gun-toting roughneck from the other day," she quips, lifting her hand and motioning toward me with her fingers that are covered in diamond jewelry. "And his goons."

There's the glint of sunshine off something in her other hand, drawing my attention, and I see her gun.

Pike and Mammoth step into the room, flanking me with their guns drawn too.

"You're outnumbered, Madeline," I tell her, holding my aim steady and my voice even. "Don't even think about whatever crazy-ass thing you have floating around in that Hollywood head of yours."

"You two deserve each other," she snarls, eyes flickering to her daughter. "Trash begets trash."

I grunt, doing everything I can mentally not to pop her in the leg for kicks.

"Ma'am," Mammoth says at my right. "He's a much nicer guy than me. I would've already shot the lot of you and given no fucks or shed any tears as you gasped for your last breath."

"The cops are almost here," Pike adds with his arm outstretched, finger hovering over the trigger of his Glock 43. "There's no escape."

I keep my gun pointed at Jamison, knowing the guys have Madeline covered. I'm pretty sure, even at this close range, she's a shit shot.

"You're worthless." She turns her venom on Jamison. "You had one job to do, and you couldn't even do it correctly. They're here because of you."

"We're here because of her." I tick my chin toward Jo. "Couldn't care less about the rest of you, but I told you before and I'll say it again, you do not get to do bad shit to her. She's mine, and I, along with my family, protect what's ours."

Madeline cackles. "She sounds like property."

"You're the one who treats her like property. To me, she's the most precious of things. You don't deserve her love or another moment of her life," I tell Madeline, but I keep my gaze pinned on Jamison.

"Shoot him already," Mammoth mutters at my side. "Let's get this shit over with."

Jamison slowly lowers Jo to the floor. "Promise me you're not going to shoot me if I let her go."

"I won't," I promise. "But you have three seconds before you take one in the head."

His eyes widen, and his arm immediately slips away

from her body. She runs toward me, slamming into my body with so much force, I stumble back a step.

The bang of a gun goes off, and Jo stiffens in my arms at the sound of a loud thud. She tips her head up and follows my gaze to where she was just standing.

"Fuck. You shot me!" Jamison screeches from the floor, rolling around.

"I never promised I wouldn't shoot you," Mammoth laughs. "Son of a bitch deserved that shit."

"Call an ambulance. I could die."

"It's your fucking leg. You aren't dying, you miserable bastard," Mammoth adds, his smile growing wider. "Fuckin' pussy."

Madeline drops her gun to the floor and steps back, looking like a trapped animal resigned to her fate.

"Well, fuck," my dad mutters, entering the room behind us. "That escalated quicker than I thought."

"I couldn't help it. Sometimes you have to take shit into your own hands," Mammoth tells him.

"Babe, you okay?" I ask, glancing down at my girl wrapped tightly around me.

She peers up at me, her blue eyes filled with tears. "I'm as okay as I can be. Better now that you're here."

"This is some fucked-up shit," I hiss.

"I know," she says, her mouth pulling down at the corners. "But you came."

"I'll always come for you," I promise. "Always."

"Get her out of here," Dad demands, touching my shoulder as he stalks by us. "We got this. James and I will handle the cops. The sheriff and I go way back."

"Come on," I command, speaking softly to Jo. "Let's get you out of here."

She clings to me, her legs wobbling on the very first step. I bend down, scooping her into my arms, knowing the shock of everything is kicking in.

"I got you, babe. Ain't going to let nothing bad happen to you."

She places her head on my chest, curling into me and crying quietly. "You saved me," she whimpers into my T-shirt. "You saved me."

I hold her tighter, keeping her secure against my body as I make my way down the hallway toward the elevator. "I'll never let you go without a fight. Move heaven and earth to find you and do everything I can to save you, even if it costs me my last breath."

She tips her head back, her blue eyes locking with mine. "I love you," she admits, her cheeks wet and eyes glossy, as she reaches up and touches my cheek.

"I love you, babe. That crazy, wild kind of love that makes a man do dumb shit. Never loved a person the way I love you either. Fucked me up right from the start."

"I'm sorry."

"I'm not." I lean forward, placing my lips on hers for a moment until the elevator door opens.

She winces as I pull my mouth away.

"What's wrong? Did he hurt you?"

"He hit me with the gun, and my head is pounding."

If I wouldn't go to jail, I'd go back and beat his ass within an inch of his life, gunshot wound, or no gunshot. He deserved so much worse than he got for laying his hands on her.

"I'll take care of you," I promise as the doors close and I take my girl home.

HER EYES FLUTTER open as I sit down on the bed next to her. "Hey." She smiles sweetly.

I brush the hair away from her forehead, exposing her temple and the bruise. "How's your head feeling?"

"Still hurts, but not as bad."

"I brought you ice to help with the swelling and bruising."

She winces as I place the pack near the spot that's already changed shades. "Thank you."

"It's ice, sweetheart," I tell her, speaking softly, knowing she probably has a headache worse than any hangover she's ever experienced in her life.

"No." She places her hand on my arm. "For everything. For coming after me. For rescuing me. For saving me. I don't know what..." Her fingers tighten against my arm, and her eyes fill with tears.

"Shh, Jo. You're safe. Nothing will hurt you here," I promise her.

The tears spill over her light eyelashes, sliding down her cheeks and falling to the pillow. "I know that.

I feel that. I don't think I've ever felt so safe in all my life."

I slide closer, resting my back against the headboard. She moves, curling into me as I lift my arm. "That's fucked up, babe."

"I know." She places her head on my stomach, sliding her fingers under the edge of my T-shirt. "But it's the truth."

"Guess Hollywood isn't as glamorous as they make it seem."

She peers up, a sad smile on her face as her fingertips drift underneath my shirt to stroke my stomach. "Every ounce of it is fake, even family."

"I can't imagine living like that."

"Nick." Her eyes lock on mine as she tilts her head back, giving me a full view of her face. "Can I ask you something, and you promise you won't think I'm totally insane?"

Moving the ice back to her temple, adjusting for her movement, I smile softly at her and say, "Always."

"Would it be okay if I stayed here? Not here, here," she adds, speaking faster than before. "But in this town. I don't want to go back to Hollywood, dodging the paparazzi everywhere I go. There's nothing for me there. No friends. No family. Nothing. But here—"

I place my finger against her lips, stopping her from going on. "Babe, I thought the whole 'I love you' talk made it pretty fucking clear where you were meant to be and stay."

Her eyes widen, and her lips part behind my index finger as she sucks in a breath. "I thought you..."

"Thought I what?"

"I thought you were saying that in the heat of the moment."

"Were you?" I ask her.

"No, of course not. I meant every word," she whispers, her beautiful blue eyes staring into mine.

"Then why would I be different?" I lift an eyebrow.

She shrugs her one shoulder that's not tucked next to me. "I don't know. I figured since you were a—"

"Don't start with the 'you're a man' bullshit. I say what I mean and mean what I say."

"Okay. So, then you're good with me getting a place and staying?"

I let her words move around my mind, soaking into me. "No. I'm not okay with that."

Her smile falls. "But you..."

"You're going to get your own place?" I ask.

"Well...I..." She blinks, gawking at me.

"Babe, you've been in my bed for days. My sheets smell like you now, which is a nice change. Your shit's all over my house. My counter in the bathroom has never had so many little tubes of whatever that shit is. You're already here. I don't know why you'd want to go anywhere else."

"Wait," she says, pushing herself up into a sitting position but leaves her one hand on my stomach. "You want me to live with you?"

"Uh, yeah, Jo. What the fuck else?"

She lifts her hand to her mouth and chews on her thumbnail. "I don't know if it's a good idea. So much could go wrong."

"I can make the spare bedroom up for you so you have your own space. Hell, use both spare bedrooms. One we can make into a giant walk-in closet, and the other can be a study or office for you to do whatever the hell you do in LA."

Her cheeks turn pink. "Well, I really don't do much in LA besides charity events and attending Hollywood parties."

"My grandparents run a charity organization. I'm sure they'd love to have you on board."

"They do?" she asks, looking shocked.

I nod. "They're loaded, but they love helping the community. My aunt Mia too. She's had a medical clinic for years to help the underserved and less financially fortunate members of our community."

"How were you born into all this goodness? You don't know how lucky you are."

"Oh. I do. Trust me. I know I was blessed the day I was born a Gallo. So, it's settled, then?"

"Which part?" she asks, sliding her hand a little farther up my T-shirt, raking her nails across my skin.

"All of it. You movin' here and staying with me. The closet. The office or whatever. Us."

Her face gets all soft and sweet. "You're going to regret this," she teases.

"Probably," I tell her, reaching underneath her and lifting her on top of me.

As soon as her middle lands on my dick, I know there's going to be a lot of upside to having Jo around forever.

22

JO

One Month Later

"Who the hell are these people?" Kimberly asks, leaning into me. "It's like you hit the hotness jackpot out here."

"I know." My smile couldn't be any bigger as I punch her shoulder.

"I mean, this is Florida, for fuck's sake, and we're in the middle of nowhere. Do they have a hotness breeding farm around here that I missed on the drive?"

"It's the genes, girl."

Her gaze dips to the crotch of Mammoth. "Them's some impressive genes too," she whispers.

"Kimberly. Stop it. That's Tamara's husband."

Her eyes widen, and she throws up her hands. "What? There's no law against looking, and I don't know Tamara from the next person."

"Tamara will rip those extensions right out of your head."

Kimberly pales, quickly turning her eyes somewhere else. "She sounds lovely."

"She is a lovely person, but in this family, you don't mess with anyone's man—or woman, for that matter."

"That sounds hot too."

"It is," I tell her, sounding like a weirdo schoolgirl with a crush.

In many ways, Nick has that edge to him. He doesn't let anyone walk all over him, but he never threatens people or is cruel. Not unless they deserve that treatment, like Jamison and my mother.

"Hey there," Rocco, one of Izzy and James's twins, says, giving Kimberly a chin lift followed quickly by a wink as he walks by. "How you doin'?"

Kimberly has always been a no-bullshit person and is used to putting up with some of the most arrogant and self-centered human beings, so Rocco Gallo stands no chance. "Have you been watching *Friends*, little boy?" Kimberly laughs.

He lifts his arm, flexing his muscles for show, and slides his hand back through his floppy black hair. "Sweetheart, there's nothing little about me."

"I don't date or flirt with minors," she tells him, crossing her arms over her chest as we stand in the driveway of Nick's house, which is now also mine too.

"I'm nineteen. Totally legal, baby." He smirks, raising

his arm higher, exposing his perfectly tanned abs along with a happy trail.

"Cocky fucker," she teases, shaking her head.

"Rocco—" Mello, his twin brother, smacks him in the back of the head "—leave the poor woman alone."

Rocco turns, glaring at Mello. "Dude, she look poor to you?"

Kimberly glances at me, and I shrug, unable to hold back my laughter. "Men."

"Girl, don't even get me started," she mutters.

"No, dumbass," Mello replies, grabbing the last box out of the moving truck. "But she's way too classy for an asshole like you."

"I clean up well, and I bet she knows how to get dirty," Rocco replies, giving Kimberly another wink.

"Oh lord," she mutters. "You sure you want to stay here?"

"I thought you said they were hot," I tease her, still laughing.

She loops her arm with mine and moves me toward the front of the house, leaving Carmello and Rocco behind. "They are, but Jo, these people are..."

"Unbelievably kind. Completely loving. Welcoming. Warm. Everything my mother and my life in California aren't," I remind her, earning me a quick nod in response because she knows how my life was. "But these men..." I smile as soon as my eyes find Nick, hauling my desk down the hallway with Pike. They're both shirtless, the material hanging from their back pockets, and looking all kinds of delicious. "They're the absolute best, along with the entire family. I've been surrounded by so much bad, I'm not giving this up for anything, including the glamour of Hollywood."

"There aren't any red carpets here. Nowhere to wear your designer gowns."

"Ah. That's where you're wrong. I'm going to be working at the Gallo Family Charity as head of donor acquisition and retention."

"Oh," she says, her eyebrows rising.

"I plan to put my Hollywood contacts to good use, and I'm also in charge of planning local events to help highlight achievements in the community."

"That sounds really lovely, Jo."

Nick stalks down the hallway, his gaze searching the people-filled living room until his eyes find mine. "Babe."

"Be back," I tell her, patting her hand before unlocking our arms. "What's up, honey buns?"

"Honey buns," Mammoth mutters as he leans against the counter in the kitchen, ankles crossed, sipping a beer. "Fuckin' priceless."

Nick turns his head, narrowing his eyes as he points at Mammoth. "Shut it."

I slide my hand up his bare chest, not giving two shits he's covered in sweat, until my fingers touch his face. With a little pressure, I get his eyes back on me. "What did you need, babe?" I say, using his word back at him instead of another term like sweet cheeks.

The attitude he was giving Mammoth vanishes the

moment he faces me. The glare is replaced by a smile, and his gaze softens. "You want the desk by the window or in the middle of the room?"

He looks extra hot with his hair all over the place, covered in the right amount of sweat to make his body glisten. I've never been attracted to a sweaty human being before, doing everything possible to avoid coming in contact with them, but Nick's different. There hasn't been a thing about him that turns me off, even when he's talking like a caveman.

I blink, confused. "That's what you wanted?"

He reaches around, cupping my ass. "The thing weighs a ton. I want it right before the guys leave."

"Middle of the room." I brush my lips against his as he squeezes my butt.

"Good call," he says, smiling down at me like I'm the very reason he breathes. "As soon as we're finished, I'm kicking everyone out."

"You are?"

His smile widens. "My girl's been in Cali for a week, and I've missed her. I need a lot of Jo time."

I snake my arms around his shoulders, shoving my fingers in the back of his hair. "Would that involve us being naked?" I whisper.

"You can bet your sweet ass, it does."

"I'm out," Kimberly proclaims, raising her hands high in the air as her stilettos click against the hardwood. "I'm going to the beach. I'll be back tomorrow."

"Want company?" Rocco asks as she moves toward the doorway where he's standing, never giving up.

"You better keep your cute ass here, kid. I'm in no mood," she tells him, giving him a little tap on the chest with her finger.

He turns, watching her sashay out the door, her hips swaying in her tight jeans. "Fuck. I think I'm in love," he mutters, covering the spot her finger had been.

"Oh Jesus," I groan. "He's ridiculous."

"At that age, all I did was..."

I cover Nick's mouth. "Don't say it."

He laughs, his eyes twinkling in the sunshine streaming through the bank of sliding glass windows behind me. "Say what?" he asks as I drop my hand.

"Exactly."

"All the shit off the truck?" he calls out to Rocco, still holding my ass as we stand plastered together.

"Yep." Rocco glances out the doorway toward the driveway. "You need me anymore? I have something to do."

"No. We're done here," Nick tells him.

Just as Rocco peels himself away from the doorframe, Carmello is at his side. "Come on, asshole. You're not chasing after her. Get that shit out of your head."

"Dude, don't ruin my night."

"I have something even better. Carrie and I are heading up to the cabin for a few days, and she invited one of her friends." Carmello waggles his dark eyebrows with a smirk. "You in?"

"Is she hot?" is Rocco's response.

Carmello stares at his brother and then smacks him in the chest. "Carrie doesn't have ugly friends."

Rocco moves his head from side to side like he's mulling it over because the decision is so hard. "Someone from high school?"

"No, dipshit. It's one of her sorority sisters. Now, get your ass moving because if I'm late, I'm going—"

"Fuck. I'm in," Rocco replies, suddenly filled with excitement. "Let's go, but I'm driving. You drive like an old woman."

"Fuck you," Carmello snaps. "I drive better."

"Still not happening," Rocco tells him, shaking his head.

"Bye," I call as they head out the door, moving quickly toward Rocco's car. "Have fun."

"Wear a fuckin' rubber," Nick yells out to his horny younger cousins.

"We're out," Pike announces, with Mammoth right behind him. "We put the desk in the middle of the room. Our women are waiting for us, and it looks like you have your hands full for the evening."

"Have fun, honey buns," Mammoth tells Nick with a smirk.

"We're alone." I peer up at him with those eyes that tell him I'm having all kinds of sinful thoughts. "And the boxes can wait."

"Have you missed me, babe?"

I slide my hand up to his face, scraping my fingers

against his scruff. "So freaking much my body aches for you."

"We better rectify that, then." He kisses the corner of my mouth but doesn't give me exactly what I want.

I press my breasts to his chest, plastering myself against him. "I could really use a shower. Care to join me?" I ask as I pull away, sliding out of his grip and slowly walking backward toward the hallway.

He watches me in sheer fascination as I lift my shirt over my head, dropping it to the floor. He takes a step toward me, only stopping when I reach for the button of my shorts.

I shimmy the material down my legs and then step out, leaving them a few feet away from my shirt. He moves faster now, removing his clothes as he follows me down the hallway to the master bedroom.

By the time he makes it to the bathroom, I have the water already running and am standing there in nothing more than my delicate black lace underwear and bra.

"How did I get so lucky?" he asks me, reaching out to pull me close and kiss my lips while the water warms.

I tip my head back, placing my hand against his chest, and look up at him like he's everything I've ever wanted. "It's all about this," I say, sliding my other hand between us and grabbing his dick. "It holds your superpowers."

He sucks in a breath as I stroke his length. "A week felt like an eternity, Josephine."

"I'm here now, Nicholas, and I'm not going anywhere," I promise him.

"You may get sick of me."

My hand moves faster, squeezing his cock harder. "Do you love me?"

"I love you," he tells me.

"More than anyone?" I ask, needing the reassurance.

"More than anyone ever."

I pull him into the shower by his cock, and he moves with me step by step under the warm spray. He presses me against the cold tile. I gasp, but he quickly muffles the sound by covering my mouth with his.

His hands slide across my slippery skin, exploring every inch of me like he's memorizing every dip and swell. He dips his tongue into my mouth, savoring the sweet taste of me.

I moan, shoving my fingers into his hair and holding his face to mine, deepening our kiss. His hands move to my back, skating down the ridge of my spine to my ass, cupping my cheeks in his hands again. As if on cue and without any words, I give him my weight, wrapping my legs around his body, using the shower wall to keep myself upright.

"Fuck me, baby," I plead.

"Condom," he mumbles.

"I'm on the pill."

"You sure about this?" he asks.

"I'm sure," I promise, against his lips. "Never been more sure about anything or anyone in my life."

With those words, he reaches between us, rubbing

the head of his shaft against my middle, and I'm dying for him to be inside me.

"Don't go slow," I beg. "I want to feel owned."

He smirks, loving when I talk that way to him. Without being gentle, he thrusts his cock inside me, slamming my back into the wall and stealing my breath.

I gasp, tightening my arms around his shoulders and pulling the strands of his hair harder with my fingers. "Yes! Just like that."

Holding my ass, he pounds into me with his hard cock.

The sex is frenzied.

My hands are moving everywhere, my nails raking over his skin, sending goose bumps along my skin as he tips his head down, dragging his lips across the swell of my breasts. He raises me higher in the air to thrust harder and deeper.

I pant with each pump as my thighs tighten around his waist, and I dig my heels into his ass, wanting and needing more.

Within seconds, his breathing changes, and he follows me into bliss as the waves of pleasure splash over us, taking us over the cliff.

23

NICK

My father greets us at the door, looking like he always does...chill. "Hey, kids," he says with a warm smile.

"Hey, Dad." I reach out and wrap an arm around him, followed by a quick pat.

He does the same before turning his gaze to Jo. "It's great to see you too, sweetheart."

Her smile can't be any bigger as he opens his arms to her completely, not going in for a bro hug. "It's always wonderful to see you, Mr. Gallo."

"Thomas or Pop, Jo. No more Mr. Gallo. I think we're past that point."

"Tommy?" she asks, peering up at him with a smirk.

"Whatever you want," he tells her, surprising me as much as her.

"Old Man works too," I add, earning myself a deadly glare from my pop.

"Honey, let the kids in!" Mom yells from inside the house. "Don't let all the air conditioning out."

My father rolls his eyes. "All I hear about is the air conditioning, and it's freezing cold in here. Damn hot flashes," he mutters.

"Hot what?" I ask.

Jo touches my arm, giving me a small smile. "It's a woman's thing, sweetie."

"Someday, you'll get to experience the joys, my son." Dad laughs, moving to the side so we can make our way into the house.

"Oh, you two look absolutely adorable," Mom says with her hands covered in oven mitts. "I've been cooking up a storm. I hope you brought your appetites."

"I'm starving," I answer as Jo kicks off her sandals, leaving them at the door with the other shoes. "Jo hasn't eaten all day either."

My mother's eyes widen. "You two really need to stop and eat sometimes. It's not healthy, and we need to make sure your body"—these words she says to Jo—"has all the vitamins it needs."

My eyebrows furrow, and I turn my head to face Jo. She's white as a ghost, blinking at my mother with her lips set in a firm line.

"Is there something I don't know?" I ask, reaching out and grabbing Jo's hand. "Anything at all?"

Jo shakes her head. "Um, no. Not that I know of, unless your mom has some weird voodoo skills."

My mom laughs, her red hair swaying. "I'm thinking about the future."

"Far. Far. Far in the future," I correct her.

"Sometimes kids sneak up on you," Dad adds like kids magically appear out of nowhere.

I pull Jo toward the couch next to my father's favorite chair and settle in with her at my side. "Did I sneak up on you?"

My dad sits, glancing over at my mother, who smiles. "You were planned."

"You sure about that?" I ask again because the way they're looking at each other says otherwise.

"Planned. Completely planned."

"But accidents do happen," Mom adds, moving back toward the kitchen island.

"Do you need help, Mrs. Gallo?" Jo asks, tangling her fingers in mine against my knee.

"You sit and relax, baby. I got this," she replies, glancing up from a pot to smile at us. "I made Nick's favorite."

"And that would be?" I ask.

I was blessed not to grow up in Gigi's house, with Suzy as a mother. For as sweet as she is, she is the worst cook in the entire world. Gigi's skills aren't far off from her mother's either.

"Homemade meatballs and ravioli from your favorite store in St. Pete."

"You went to Mazzaro's?" My stomach instantly

grumbles, begging for a piece of the heaven that lies within those pots.

"Of course," Mom says, stirring the sauce. "Always the best for you kids."

"I get frozen ravioli," Dad tells Jo and then tips his head to me. "But when he comes over for dinner, she'll drive an hour each way to get him his favorite."

"Stop whining," Mom tells Dad, giving him a wink when he glances over his shoulder to look at her. "I spoil you in other ways."

Jo giggles, knowing exactly what they're talking about, but I can only shake my head, still not comfortable thinking about my parents having sex.

"You two are trying to kill me," I mumble.

When I was little, I walked in on them. Took me almost five years to get that visual out of my head every time I looked them in the eye. Wrestling was never the same either. I immediately left the team, finding the sport way too sexual and the memory too much for me to shake.

"Any trouble from the press lately?" Dad asks Jo when he finally turns back around, thankfully changing the subject.

Jo scoots closer, pressing her side against me. "Not really. I take too many selfies and other photos to post on my social media. There's not much else they can get that I don't share myself. I took the power out of their hands."

"Smart girl," he praises her, smiling.

"I listened to what you said, Mr...."

Dad raises an eyebrow.

"Thomas," Jo corrects herself quickly. "They're too busy following my mother's court dates and cases, along with Jamison's, to worry about me walking around barefoot on the beach. There's no need for them to be way out here when there are no other celebrities for hundreds of miles."

"It's a slice of heaven, isn't it?" Dad asks her.

"It is." She smiles, squeezing my hand. "I never knew I could find such peace."

"Dad, I was wondering if, tomorrow after dinner at Grandma's, you'd go with Jo and me to the range. I want her to learn how to handle a weapon and shoot."

My father's eyebrows rise again. "You don't want to teach her?"

I shake my head. "I think you'd be better at it. You taught me everything I know, and you have way more patience than I do, too. I can teach her the basics, but you're better with the mechanics."

"You want to learn?" Dad asks her, going right by me.

"Yes. I was never allowed to handle a gun before, but now, I feel like I need to at least know how to protect myself in case anything happens to me again."

"Are you going to carry?" he asks Jo.

Her forehead wrinkles. "Carry?"

"Conceal and carry. You can get a permit to carry a gun in your purse or hidden on your person."

Jo blinks. "Oh, no. I don't want to carry it everywhere."

Dad laughs softly. "We'll see how you feel after tomorrow. You've been through a lot, and although you're no longer in Cali, I worry you'll always be a target, even a small one, for creepers who are fascinated with your mother."

Jo pulls her lip in her mouth, chewing on the corner. I reach up, releasing the strong hold and rescuing that small patch of skin before she gnaws it away. "Baby, you're safe here. Don't worry. Dad's always overcautious about everything."

"Don't listen to my husband, Jo. In his line of work, he's always thinking about the worst-case scenario. He always goes overboard."

"Babe," Dad says, reaching back as my mother tries to walk by him and snagging her around the legs. He hauls her into his lap like two teenagers in love. "Even you got into some shit, yeah?"

"Yes, Thomas," she says with so much attitude.

"I saved you, didn't I?"

"Yes."

"Could you have saved yourself?"

"No." She rolls her eyes. "You'll never let me forget it either, will you?"

He nuzzles his face into her neck, hugging her tight. "Could you save yourself now?"

She sags against him. "I could, but only because you taught me how to protect myself after, you know...."

"Right, baby. Every person, man or woman, should know what to do in case someone comes after them or puts their life in danger," Dad replies, stroking my mother's arm with his thumb.

"What's 'you know'?" Jo asks, and my mother straightens. "If it's none of my business, please tell me to shut up."

"No, darling. I don't mind talking about what happened to me. It was a long time ago, before Nicholas was born."

I pull Jo tighter against me with my arm around her shoulder, our other hands still locked together. "My parents had a wild past."

"We did." Dad smiles, tipping his head back to look at my mom. "I'm glad we made it out, but it was close and nothing I'd like to relive."

"I know, sweetie," she agrees, touching his cheek before turning her gaze toward Jo. "We met on the job. Thomas was undercover with a motorcycle club, working for the government, and I was working at an establishment owned by the same club. Well, after we broke free and Thomas brought me home with him, we thought we were done. But someone had other plans."

"Oh God," Jo gasps. "Did they hurt you?"

"No. Thomas got to me in time and rescued me. He was and always has been my personal hero."

"Like father, like son," Jo whispers at my side, her gaze flickering between my father and me. "Was it love at first sight?" she goes on to ask, but I already know the answer is probably going to blow her mind.

My mother laughs. "It was lust at first sight, for sure.

The way he looked at me..." Mom fans herself. "I knew I wanted a piece of him."

"Baby, you make me sound like a piece of meat. I should be offended."

Mom slaps Dad playfully, and I turn, seeing Jo's smile and ease around my parents.

Jo loves them. She loves their sweetness, something I took for granted growing up in a household filled with love. She, on the other hand, never knew and would never know what that was like for a kid and how it shaped my views.

"I'm pretty sure I was the prey, sweetie," Mom tells him, gently pressing her lips against his cheek. "And I was okay with that."

Jo leans over, placing her mouth next to my ear. "I love your parents," she whispers.

There's a knock at the door, and every head in the room turns to face it.

"It's James and Izzy. I invited them for dinner tonight." Mom springs up from Dad's lap and heads toward the door.

"My aunt and uncle," I tell Jo.

"I remember," she replies, smiling at me. "I love that there are always a lot of people. Years of being alone was awful, and it's nice to be surrounded by so many."

"Sometimes togetherness is overrated, babe."

She swats at me. "Stop with the lies, Nicholas. You love being around your family."

I lean over this time with my lips touching her ear.

"Sometimes being alone is better," I say, speaking slow and low. "Especially when you're naked in my bed."

Jo blushes. "Stop talking about being naked with your immaculate body."

"Don't forget my pierced cock, babe." I smile against her skin.

She turns to face me until our lips are lined up. "You play so dirty," she whispers, her eyes dilated and breathing slower.

Although I love my family, I'd much rather be at home, naked wrestling with my girl in our bed. It's weird to think it's not my bed anymore, but ours. The first time ever I've had a woman living with me, and so far, it hasn't been bad. For as spoiled as she was growing up, she's pretty damn easygoing with most things...except her clothes and shoes, but there's nothing I can do about that now. My aunts and girl cousins are no different, and I know better than to even try to change Jo.

"Well, look at you two lovebirds," Aunt Izzy says as she steps into the living room, with James right behind her.

Her brown hair is swept up in a loose bun, makeup done perfectly as always because she never leaves the house without putting her "face on"...whatever that means.

Mom grabs Izzy's arm, staring at Jo and me like we're a circus attraction. "Aren't they adorable?"

"They're going to make beautiful babies." Those words come from my aunt.

"Oh, well... It's a bit early for that," Jo replies. "I plan to enjoy Nick as much as possible before we even talk about babies."

Izzy twists her lips and then bursts into laughter. "You're too cute. I wasn't ready for a baby either, but bam, Rocco and Carmello happened."

James wraps his arms around my aunt in that strong, possessive way he always does. "It was all part of my plan."

She glances over her shoulder, narrowing her eyes. "I love my boys, but I wasn't ready."

"No one ever is, baby."

"That's the truth." She lifts her shoulders, moving into his touch as James kisses her neck. "But I love our boys more than life itself."

"More than me?" James asks, pretending to be offended.

"Don't be silly," she teases, turning in his arms and tipping her head toward his face as he slides his hands to her ass. "Of course, I love them more."

He swats one of her cheeks, causing her to laugh. "Well, you asked, and I'm always truthful."

"God, they're so dreamy, too," Jo breathes. "They're like every perfect Hollywood story I always thought was only possible in movies, but never real life."

"He's a complete pain in the ass," Izzy says without turning around to face us and overhearing Jo. "No man is easy."

"The same could be said about you, love," James

replies, staring down at his wife with nothing but love and admiration.

"Was it love at first sight for you, too?" Jo asks, so curious about my family and the depth and easiness with which they love.

Izzy throws her head back and laughs loudly. "I hated James."

"Baby, you slept with me the first night. You didn't hate me all that much."

"I was drunk."

"Easy out."

"You were a cocky prick."

"Still am, but that's why you love me so much."

"You slept with your best friend's sister. You clearly had no morals or boundaries," she adds.

James smirks. "The moment I laid eyes on you, I knew I had to make you mine. I didn't care that Thomas was my best friend. I spent years listening to him talk about his little sister and how great she was. I couldn't help that he already had you in my head before I ever met you. The other stuff, after we first met, that was the icing on the cake. I love a woman with some bite to her."

"Dinner's ready. Who's hungry?" Mom asks, back at the stove, missing out on another trip down memory lane.

"I'll pour the wine," Izzy announces, sliding out of James's grip.

"I really do love the women in this family," Jo says, moving away from me too and following behind Izzy.

"You're shot," James tells me as I stare at Jo, not

missing the sway of her hips or the grace with which she carries herself across the room.

My eyes slide to him, and I furrow my forehead. "Excuse me?"

"You're in love, kid. You may think you're only playing house, but she's deep in you. Part of you now. There's no getting away from that."

"I wasn't planning on getting away."

"You going to marry her?" Dad asks me, speaking quietly so the women don't overhear.

"One step at a time," I lie. "I don't want to get ahead of myself."

I very much plan to put a ring on her finger. And the sooner, the better.

"Whatever lie you need to tell yourself, son."

24

JO

It's Sunday, which means great food, the entire family, and tons of love.

The women are gathered in the living room at Nick's grandparents' house as the men head outside to watch the game on the television hanging on the lanai.

That's a new word I learned since moving to Florida. In California, we said patio or terrace, but here, it's all about the lanai. Most of them are screened-in, including the pool, and with the numbers of critters around here, it's absolutely perfect.

"What's your best advice for us, Nana?" Gigi asks, sitting on the floor near her grandmother's feet, one arm resting on the edge of the cushion. "How have you and Grandpa stayed married and together for so long?"

Her grandmother touches Gigi's brown hair, staring down at her granddaughter like she's the most precious thing in the world. "There's no one thing, baby. It's a mixture of many things, depending on the situation or level of anger."

"But you don't get angry with Grandpa," Lily adds, sitting on the couch across the room with her legs folded underneath her. "At least, I've never seen it."

Their grandmother laughs. She's so beautiful with her silver-white hair and beautiful clothes. But the most beautiful thing of all is the way she is devoted to and loves her family. "Baby, I get mad at him daily, but after being together over fifty years, you learn how to *handle* a person."

Tamara snickers. "I can't believe you're saying you *handle* Grandpa."

Mrs. Gallo tips her nose upward, looking very regal in her high-back chair made for a queen. "Well, I do. Sometimes the truth hurts or is hard to believe, but I do, in fact, *handle* the man, as I do each of my children."

"That's no shit," Izzy mumbles behind me. "She's still the boss."

"As women, we're the thread that holds the fabric of this family together. Without us, the entire thing would unravel. No one would be here today. We wouldn't be sitting around like this, sharing a meal, and enjoying one another's company. Someday, when I'm gone—"

"Nana, you aren't going anywhere," Tamara interrupts, shaking her head. "Stop that right now."

Her grandmother gives her a sad yet sweet smile. "Not right now, but someday, I won't be here. Many years from now, you'll be sitting in this chair, surrounded by your children and grandchildren, hopefully handing down the same advice I am giving to you, child."

"I'm not ready for that." Tamara pulls her knees against her chest and rests her chin on top. "I need you here. We all do."

"I'm here, sweetie." Mrs. Gallo smiles, but she rarely doesn't, at least not in the few weeks I've known her. "But I need to pass down my words of wisdom, so when I do leave this earth, I know y'all won't be walking around clueless."

"Oh dear God," Fran, Mrs. Gallo's sister-in-law, mutters. "Get on with it, Marie. You're talking in circles, repeating yourself. I may literally take my last breath before you dole out this wisdom."

Everyone chuckles, and Mrs. Gallo, in a surprising move, at least to me, holds up her middle finger. "Have another drink, Fran. Do something constructive with that mouth instead of giving me sass."

Fran scoots forward and holds up her hand too, but not her middle finger. "Let me give my advice first. I have words of wisdom too, especially after two very different husbands."

"Go ahead, Fran. You have the floor," Mrs. Gallo offers, waving her hand toward her sister-in-law. "I'm waiting with bated breath for this special knowledge you're going to impart to the younger generation."

Fran quickly rolls her eyes before sitting forward, crossing her legs, and placing her hands on her knees. "First, exhaust him in the sack."

"Oh Jesus," Mrs. Gallo mutters, covering her face with her hands. "Here we go."

I chuckle, loving the dynamic of the entire family. I wonder how I'd be different if I'd grown up surrounded by loving, strong women and equally strong and devoted men. Being surrounded instead by people hired to care for you leaves marks that can't be seen on the surface but are permanently etched under my skin.

"Don't act like Mother Teresa, Marie, and don't pretend you haven't used your sex skills to get exactly what you want from Sal."

There's a collective groan, but I can't wipe the stupid smile off my face.

"I still remember the French maid outfit incident. I do believe that happened because you were trying to make Sal more agreeable."

"Drop it," Mrs. Gallo tells her.

"Please don't remind me about that day," Izzy says. "I've never been more embarrassed and horrified at the same time."

"Says the girl with the collar," Max, her sister-in-law, mutters. "I'm pretty sure you've been in more embarrassing situations." Izzy elbows Max in the ribs, causing her to jerk sideways and wince. "Fuck, I was kidding, bitch. Calm down."

"Sal's mother gave us the best advice when we were young like you kids," Mrs. Gallo says, taking the conversation away.

"I loved my mom, but she was old-school," Fran tells

Marie. "God rest her soul." Fran taps her forehead, her chest, and then each shoulder. "She was an amazing woman, but she believed in subservience and would probably disown us if she could see us today."

Mrs. Gallo nods, laughing. "She was a little over the top. I mean, she wore nothing but black for two decades after your father passed."

"Twenty years wasted. If Bear dies, I'll allow myself one year to mourn before I go back on the prowl."

As if on cue, her husband, Bear, pokes his head into the room. "You talkin' about me, woman?"

Fran's head snaps to the side, and the biggest smile covers her face. "Just sayin' how much I love you, babe."

He studies her, his eyes sweeping across her face. "You're lying."

She touches her chest and gasps, keeping her eyes trained on him. "How dare you? I never lie."

Those words get a grunt out of him, followed by a muttered *bullshit,* before he vanishes as quickly as he arrived.

"Aunt Fran," Tamara says when we're all alone again. "Can I ask you something?"

Fran nods, still laughing at what happened with Bear. "Of course, dear."

"Why do you always feel up every man who walks into this house? I mean, we expect it. We accept it, but why? Uncle Bear is pretty damn hot, especially for his age."

"Oh dear," Mrs. Gallo mutters.

Fran laughs harder. "Babe, we may be older, but we're not dead. You make Bear sound like he's ready for the old-age home."

"Well..." Tamara shrugs. "He's not young."

"You're right, Tam. We're *older*, but we're not old. Age is a number, but youth is a frame of mind."

"Okay," Tam whispers. "I'll give you that, but what's with the dudes?"

Fran sits back, relaxing with a smile still planted on her face. "There are some good things that come with age. When I was younger, I couldn't get away with half the shit I do now. But people tend to let older people get away with more things. If I were your age and touched every man, I'd never hear the end of it."

"You'd probably get arrested," Mrs. Gallo tells her, shaking her head in judgment.

"Maybe." Fran shrugs. "Wouldn't be my first time in jail."

"What?" Izzy says quickly, turning to face her aunt. "Why haven't I heard this story?"

"Some things are meant to be private," Fran tells her, wagging her finger toward her niece. "Anyway," she continues, skating right by the arrest, "I love men."

"Shocking," Suzy teases from the other side of the room.

Fran shoots her a glare, and Suzy quickly quiets, something I've noticed since the moment I met her. She's the quietest of all the women. Still strong, but easily swayed or silenced when pushed. It's not hard with the number of strong and overly vocal females in this family.

"Besides being an admirer of the male form, nothing gets Bear more worked up than him finding me touching another man. Bear has a nasty, yet sexy as hell, jealous streak. So, when he finds me touching someone else, I know I'm going to—"

"Don't finish that statement," Izzy tells her, holding up a hand. "We got it."

"So, you feel up every man to get Uncle Bear worked up?" Tamara asks for clarification.

"Yes, but chick, the men are so damn fine, I'd be a moron not to at least get one touch in when I first meet them, before they become someone's husbands. I'm old, not stupid."

"Jealousy is a great motivator," Mrs. Gallo says, agreeing with her sister-in-law. "I've used it a time or two on Sal, but never by groping other men."

"You've missed a lot of muscles, Marie. Your loss, not mine."

"This is the most ridiculous conversation ever," Max scoffs, shaking her head and finally standing. "I don't know about you ladies, but I have a man to check on."

"You carry his balls around in your purse?" Izzy asks her before she even takes a step. "Or do you give them back every once in a while?"

Max swivels around, placing her hand on her hip and dropping a shoulder. "You know your brother. Do you think he could handle having them all the time?"

Izzy instantly laughs. "Nope. No, he could not. He was nothing but trouble before you walked into his life."

"He walked into mine," Max corrects her. "Implanted himself there and then wouldn't leave."

Izzy waves her hand. "Oh, stop. You loved being chased."

Max twists her lips and slowly shakes her head. "He wore me down."

"You okay?" Gigi asks me, leaning over as I watch the two aunts going back and forth, something I see often with this family.

"I love them all so much," I tell her, giving her my full attention. "Do you know how lucky you are to have them all?"

She smiles, nodding. "I do, and I remind myself of that every day when they get on my nerves."

"Hey, babe," Nick says, sliding behind me, almost making me jump out of my skin. I'd been so focused on Gigi, I hadn't noticed him enter the room. "You okay in here?"

I lean back, giving him my weight. "I couldn't be better. I love your family, Nicky."

"They're pretty great," he whispers in my ear, holding me tight, nuzzling his face in my hair.

"The best," I correct him, turning my face until our lips meet. "Thank you."

"For what?" he asks, his blue eyes searching mine.

"For not only loving me, but for making me feel like I have a family for the first time in my life."

"It's nothing about making you feel, Jo. They are your family now, too. What's mine is yours."

"We're crazy. You know that, right?" I ask him, resting my forehead against his.

"Why?"

"We've known each other for like five weeks, and I'm completely and utterly stupid in love with you. It's insane."

"Love isn't sane, babe. It's wild. It can't be forced or contained." He reaches down, lifting my hand up. "But once you find it, you do whatever you can in order to keep it. Josephine Carmichael, will you marry me?" Something cold touches my finger as he moves it down toward my palm.

My mouth drops open and my heart sputters, almost stopping. I blink, my eyes moving from his face to my finger and back to his face. My hands start to shake, followed by the rest of me. "Nick, are you..."

Oh.

My.

God.

Is he really...

I blink, gawking at him before my eyes widen.

Did he?

Nick Gallo *is* proposing to me.

He gives me a warm smile, something that's common now. He's so different from the first night we met, when he was all cranky and short. But then again, I was a sobbing mess who couldn't even think straight.

Somehow, we changed each other. I got under his skin, and he opened up a world to me I never knew existed.

"I love you, Jo. I want you to be my wife."

"Do it," Gigi whispers at my side. "Say yes, girl."

My mouth is still agape as I stare into his unwavering blue eyes. "Yes," I whisper, my eyes filling with tears as my vision blurs.

I'd been so in shock, I hadn't noticed the room drop dead silent as every set of eyes focused on us.

"Yes," I repeat again, reaching up, not even bothering to look at the ring, to grab his face. "I want this crazy, wild love. I want you."

His lips are on mine a second later, kissing me deep and hard. I'm lost in the moment, forgetting everyone and everything around us until the catcalls start, followed by the clapping.

I back away, my face heating as I stare at my fiancé. A man I didn't know two months ago, but now can't imagine not being in my life. "Is this real?" I ask, still in shock as I stare at the princess cut diamond on my finger.

"Very real, babe. You're mine now."

"I'm yours," I promise.

"Our numbers are getting better," someone says, and I don't understand what that means, but they're all excited.

"Soon they'll be outnumbered," Max replies.

"Congratulations, sweetheart," Angel says, placing

her hand on my shoulder. "We're so happy you're officially going to be part of our family."

Those are the words that will forever be etched in my brain. Not only do I have the love of a good man, but I have a family. I finally have something I've wanted my entire life and assumed I'd never have.

"Thank you," I weep.

Nick wipes at my cheeks, drying my skin, and it only makes my crying worse. "I love you," he whispers as the family celebrates around us.

"I love you too."

"Yes, this is Isabella Caldo," Izzy says, standing next to where we're sitting. There's a long pause, and then. "Say that again?"

The room grows quiet because Izzy's joyous tone has vanished. As I tip my head back, staring up at Nick's beautiful aunt, I see the color drain from her face.

"Which one?" She squeezes her eyes shut, clutching her chest with her other hand. "Where are they?"

"What's wrong?" Nick's grandma asks, walking toward her daughter.

Izzy's hand, along with the phone, falls to her side. "There's been an accident. Carmello and Rocco were in the car."

Nick's grandma touches Izzy's shoulder. "Are they okay?"

"I don't know. They said there's one fatality, and the survivors are being transported to the hospital."

"Oh God," I whisper, covering my mouth, the happiness from a moment ago totally gone and suddenly unimportant.

"What's wrong?" James asks, rushing into the room like he has a sixth sense.

"The boys. There's been an accident."

"How bad?" he asks, his body going rigid.

"Someone's dead," she whispers so softly, I can barely hear her.

"Our boys?" he asks her, moving quickly in her direction. "Are they okay?"

"I don't know. They wouldn't tell me," she says to him as he grabs on to her, giving her the support she needs.

"Let's go, baby. They're okay. I know they're okay. You'll see," he promises her, but his body is saying the opposite.

"What if—" she starts, but he shakes his head.

"Don't," he warns her. "Don't say it, Isabella."

What if the happiest day of my life is filled with loss and sorrow and is now one of the worst for the entire family?

EPILOGUE

NICK

Five Years Later

"Rocco," I call out, waving him over. "Sit with us."

He lifts his eyes from the sand for a moment to look our way. "In a bit," he replies, but as soon as the words are out of his mouth, he drops his head down again.

Damn. The kid hasn't been the same since the accident, and it's been five years. Every day, I pray something pulls him out of the self-induced hell he's placed himself in. Maybe someone. He can't go on like this...not forever.

"Valentino, come here, baby," Jo calls out, motioning for our son as he runs across the sand in his bare feet, squealing as he chases the sea gulls.

"Leave him be," I tell her, running my hand across her giant belly. "You think we're going to have a little girl?"

She covers my hands with hers. "Feels like a girl. This

pregnancy has been so different from when I had Val growing inside me."

"It's a girl," I whisper with a smile. "I need a little you running around the house, wrapping her body around my leg, begging for my attention. I need a daddy's girl."

"Be careful what you wish for, brother," Jett tells me, dipping his head toward Celeste as she splashes in the waves with Gigi and Pike. "That one has me wrapped around her finger so hard, I'd bury a body for her without even asking a question."

"Celeste wouldn't hurt a fly," Lily argues, running her hand up and down Jett's leg. "So, you never have to worry about having to do that. But..."

"But what?" he asks her, sitting up a little straighter when she doesn't answer right away.

"Wait until she starts dating. That's going to be—" she smiles and stares across the sand at her daughter "—interesting."

"She's not dating until she's thirty," Jett tells everyone.

"Okay," Tamara snorts. "Good luck with that one."

"I'm down with that," Mammoth agrees. "No way in hell is anyone getting near Riley. I'll go to jail before any boy lays his hands on her."

Tamara smacks his shoulder. "Stop. You will not."

"Wanna bet?" he asks, lifting Riley's little body higher on his chest. Her cheek is smashed against his skin, drool pooling underneath. "No one is ever hurting my baby girl."

Tamara crosses her arms, raising an eyebrow. "What about Jackson? Will he have the same dating rules, then?"

"Princess, he's a boy." Mammoth smiles, totally missing the cues his wife is throwing his way.

"Da fuck does that mean?" She straightens, turning her ass around in the sand to face him. "Riley and Jackson are no different."

"Penis says otherwise," Mammoth jokes, but Tamara does not laugh.

"Oh boy," Jo whispers, squeezing my fingers that are still resting against her belly.

"Jackson will be a man, Tam. He'll be able to take care of himself."

"Riley will be a woman someday, but make no mistake, she'll be able to kick any man's ass. Even Jackson's."

Jackson's running after Valentino but stops when he hears his name. "Yeah?" he yells, his mess of brown curls blowing in the breeze.

"Nothing, baby. Keep playing!" Tamara yells back, shooing him with her hand.

Pike and Gigi make their way up the sand to the sea of blankets and towels we have set out.

Gigi sticks her head into the tent, checking on her little one, who's fast asleep in the shade and has been for the last hour. "What'd we miss? Looks tense up here."

"We're talking about the kids dating."

"What?" She pulls her head back out, staring at us.

"Well." Tamara ticks her head at her husband. "This

one said Jackson can have free rein because he has a dick, but Riley can't date until she's thirty."

"That's stupid." Gigi rolls her eyes. "But it's totally man logic, even if it makes no sense."

"Darlin', man logic is going to win out on this one," Pike says to her as he collapses back onto the blanket a few feet away.

"We'll see." She smirks. "Good luck controlling a teenage girl, baby."

"If they're anything like us, we're screwed," Tamara groans.

"Totally fucked," I add. "You three were hell on wheels."

"The two of them." Lily points back and forth between Tamara and Gigi. "Not me. I was an angel."

Gigi and Tamara burst into laughter.

"You were better behaved, but an angel you were not, Lily," Gigi reminds her.

"I was an angel," I add in, earning all the stares. "Fine, but I wasn't the most out of control."

Gigi purses her lips, staring at the kids as Rocco scoops them up in his arms as they squeal. "That's debatable."

"We can all agree on one thing..." I say, hugging my girl, staring at Valentino. "We all want the best for our kids, and at least they'll have one another like we did. At the end of the day, all we have is family."

I HOPE Nick made you swoon and left you with a big smile, too. Are you ready for more Gallos? The Men of Inked Heatwave continues in **Ember**...

Rocco Caldo is the guy all the women want. Tall, dark, and handsome with an edge that could cut deep if he'd let a woman get close enough to feel his sting. But all of that changes when someone from his past finds the kink in his very carefully crafted armor, exposing his heart along with his tragic past.

TAP HERE TO READ EMBER

Or visit ***menofinked.com/ember*** *for more information on the next Men of Inked Heatwave novel.*

BLISS UPDATE

Finish Date: November 9, 2020

I've found it interesting to write a small message after I finish each book, looking back at what happened during that period. It's a small chunk in time, but never uneventful...whether good or bad—especially now.

On October 16th, my grandpa passed away at the age of ninety-four. That was the biggest, most important, and saddest thing that happened while I wrote Spark. The man was everything to me and our family. I was blessed to have him the first forty-four years of my life. His face always lit up when he saw me, and I'll never forget how hard he loved me as well as his other grandchildren and three daughters. His laugh is something I will never forget. I hope he's at peace, watching over us all now.

Nothing else really happened. Hard to have anything eventful when you don't leave the house much. I bought an extra Christmas tree because it's 2020 and I might as well have two. Anything to bring more joy into this stressful world.

You'll be reading this at the start of 2021. I hope the year is better for us all than 2020 has been. It's definitely one that will be imprinted on our minds forever.

Love Always,

Chelle Bliss

THROTTLE
HOOK
RESIST
MEN OF inked
CHELLE BLISS
MENOFINKED.COM/FREE
READ FREE
Apple Books
amazon
BARNES&NOBLE
Rakuten kobo
Google Play

ABOUT Chelle Bliss

She's a full-time writer, time-waster extraordinaire, social media addict, coffee fiend, and ex-history teacher.

To learn more about her books, please visit *menofinked.com*.

Join Chelle's newsletter by visiting
menofinked.com/news

Get New Release Text Notifications (US only)
➔ Text **BLISS** to **24587**

Join her **Private Facebook Reader Group** at
facebook.com/groups/blisshangout

Where to Follow Me:

facebook.com/authorchellebliss1
bookbub.com/authors/chelle-bliss
instagram.com/authorchellebliss
twitter.com/ChelleBliss1
goodreads.com/chellebliss
amazon.com/author/chellebliss
pinterest.com/chellebliss10

View Chelle's entire collection of books at

menofinked.com/books

Original Men of Inked Series

Join the Gallo siblings as their lives are turned upside down by irresistible chemistry and unexpected love. A sizzling USA Today bestselling series!

Throttle Me - Book 1 (Free Download)

Ambitious Suzy has her life planned out, but everything changes when she meets tattooed bad boy **Joseph Gallo**. Could their one-night stand ever turn into the real thing?

Hook Me - Book 2

Michael Gallo has been working toward his dream of winning a MMA championship, but when he meets a sexy doctor who loathes violence, his plans may get derailed.

Resist Me - Book 3

After growing up with four older brothers, **Izzy Gallo** refuses to be ordered around by anyone. So when hot, bossy

James Caldo saves her from trouble, will she be able to give up control?

Uncover Me - Book 4

Roxanne has been part of the dangerous Sun Devils motorcycle club all of her life, while **Thomas Gallo** has been deep undercover for so long, he's forgotten who he truly is. Can they find redemption and save each other?

Without Me - Book 5

Anthony Gallo never thought he'd fall in love, but when he meets the only woman who doesn't fall to her knees in front of him, he's instantly smitten.

Honor Me - Book 6

Joe and Suzy Gallo have everything they ever wanted and are living the American dream. Just when life has evened out, a familiar enemy comes back to haunt them.

Worship Me - Book 7

James Caldo needs to control everything in his life, even his wife. But **Izzy Gallo**'s stubborn and is constantly testing her husband's limits as much as he pushes hers.

Men of Inked: Heatwave Series

The Next Generation

Flame - Book 1

Gigi Gallo's childhood was filled with the roar of a motorcycle and the hum of a tattoo gun. Fresh out of college, she never expected to run into someone tall, dark, and totally sexy from her not-so-innocent past.

Burn - Book 2

Gigi Gallo thought she'd never fall in love, but then he rode into her world covered in ink and wrapped in chaos. Pike Moore never expected his past to follow him into his future, but nothing stays hidden for long.

Wildfire - Book 3

Tamara Gallo knew she was missing something in life. Looking for adventure, she takes off, searching for a hot biker who can deliver more than a good time. But once inside the Disciples, she may get more than she bargained for.

Blaze - Book 4

Lily Gallo has never been a wild child, but when she reconnects with an old friend, someone she's always had a crush on, she's about to change.

Ignite - Book 5

Mammoth Saint is ready to sever ties from the club for good, choosing love over the brotherhood, until someone from his past shows up and threatens his freedom along with their future.

Spark - Book 6

Nick Gallo can't turn his back to a woman in need, but he never expected the Hollywood princess to work her way under his skin and into his heart.

Ember - Book 7

Rocco Caldo does everything he can to not get attached, but when a girl from his past walks back into his life, she maybe the only one to chase his nightmares away.

*More Men of Inked Heatwave books to come. Visit **menofinked.com/heatwave** to learn more.*

Men of Inked: Southside Series

The Chicago side of the Gallo Family

Maneuver - Book 1

Poor single mother Delilah is suspicious when sexy **Lucio Gallo** offers her and her baby a place to live. But soon the muscular bar owner is working his way into her heart — and into her bed...

Flow - Book 2

The moment **Daphne Gallo** looked into his eyes, she knew she was in trouble. Their fathers were enemies--Chicago crime bosses from rival families. But that didn't stop Leo Conti from pursuing her.

Hook - Book 3

Nothing prepared **Angelo Gallo** for losing his wife. He promised her that he'd love again. Find someone to mend his broken heart. And that seemed impossible, until the day that he walked into Tilly Carter's cupcake shop.

Hustle - Book 4

Vinnie Gallo's the hottest rookie in professional football. He's a smooth-talker, good with his hands, and knows how to score. Nothing will stop Vinnie from getting the girl—not a crazy stalker or the fear he's falling in love.

Love - Book 5

Finding love once is hard, but twice is almost impossible. **Angelo Gallo** had almost given up, but then Tilly Carter walked into his life and the sweet talkin' Southern girl stole his heart forever.

ALFA Investigations Series

A sexy, suspenseful Men of Inked Spin-off series...

Sinful Intent - Book 1

Out of the army and back to civilian life, **Morgan DeLuca** takes a job with a private investigation firm. When he meets his first client, one night of passion blurs the line between business and pleasure...

Unlawful Desire - Book 2

Frisco Jones was never lucky in love and had finally given up, diving into his new job at ALFA Investigations. But when a dirty-mouthed temptress crossed his path, he questioned everything.

Wicked Impulse - Book 3

Bear North, ALFA's resident bad boy, had always lived by the friend's code of honor—Never sleep with a buddy's sister, and family was totally off-limits. But that was before **Fran DeLuca**, his best friend's mom, seduced him.

Guilty Sin - Book 5

When a mission puts a woman under **Ret North**'s protection, he and his longtime girlfriend Alese welcome her into their home. What starts out as a friendship rooted in trust ignites into a romance far bigger than any of them expect.

Single Novels

Enshrine

Callie never liked to rely on anyone else for help—until she finds support and passion with the most notorious and dangerous man in town.

Mend

Before senior year, I was forced to move away, leaving behind the only man I ever loved. He promised he'd love me forever. He vowed nothing would tear us apart. He swore he'd wait for me, but Jack lied.

Rebound

After having his heart broken, **Flash** heads to New Orleans to lose himself, but ends up finding so much more!

Acquisition - Takeover 1

Rival CEO Antonio Forte is arrogant, controlling, and sexy as hell. He'll stop at nothing to get control of Lauren's company.The only problem? He's also the one-night stand she can't forget. And Antonio not only wants her company, he wants her as part of the acquisition.

Merger - Takeover 2

Antonio Forte has always put business before pleasure, but ever since he met the gorgeous CEO of Interstellar Corp, he finds himself wanting both. And he's hoping she won't be able to refuse his latest offer.

Top Bottom Switch

Ret North knows exactly who he is—a Dominant male with an insatiable sexual appetite. He's always been a top, searching for his bottom...until a notorious switch catches his eye.

Love at Last Series

Untangle Me - Book 1

Kayden is a bad boy that never played by the rules. **Sophia** has always been the quintessential good girl, living a life filled with disappointment. Everything changes when their lives become intertwined through a chance encounter online.

Kayden the Past - Book 2

Kayden Michaels has a past filled with sex, addiction, and heartache. Needing to get his addictions in check and gain control of his life for the sake of his family, Kayden is forced to confront his past and make amends for the path he's walked.